Major bummer

"Social services just called," Leaf stated. "We've got a new social worker, and she decided to check up on you. She talked to the school." He turned and looked me right in the eye. "Your grades are bombing big time, Blue."

At first I couldn't even process everything he'd said. We'd gotten a new social worker? How come nobody told us? I swallowed again, hard, and stared down at my shoes. There was nothing I could say either. My grades *did* stink.

"Something's gotta change, Blue," he added.

Now my heart started beating a little faster. I hadn't thought about social services in a long time. I'd forgotten about the power that they have. Leaf is my legal guardian, but child welfare has the right to check up on us and make sure I'm in an okay environment. And if they don't like what they see . . .

Well, I didn't even want to think about that.

Don't miss any of the books in SWEET VALLEY JUNIOR HIGH, an exciting series from Bantam Books!

True Blue

Written by
Jamie Suzanne

Created by
FRANCINE PASCAL

BANTAM BOOKS
NEW YORK · TORONTO · LONDON · SYDNEY · AUCKLAND

To Caroline Anne

RL 4, 008–012

TRUE BLUE

A Bantam Book / June 2000

Sweet Valley Junior High is a trademark of Francine Pascal.
Conceived by Francine Pascal.
Cover photography by Michael Segal.

Produced by 17th Street Productions,
an Alloy Online, Inc. company.
33 West 17th Street
New York, NY 10011.

ISBN: 0-553-48706-X

Visit us on the Web! www.randomhouse.com/kids

Published simultaneously in the United States and Canada

Bantam Books is an imprint of Random House Children's Books, a
division of Random House, Inc. BANTAM BOOKS and the rooster
colophon are registered trademarks of Random House, Inc. Bantam Books,
1540 Broadway, New York, New York 10036.

PRINTED IN THE UNITED STATES OF AMERICA

OPM   0 9 8 7 6 5 4 3 2 1

Elizabeth

"Incoming!" Brian Rainey yelled. He launched his paper airplane across the empty classroom toward Salvador del Valle.

But instead of flying in a line, the plane curved hard to the right—straight at my face. I ducked just in time. The plane whizzed right over my head.

"Hey!" I protested.

Brian smiled sheepishly. "Sorry."

Salvador laughed. "Good aim," he joked.

I sighed and sat up straight, frowning and brushing a few strands of blond hair out of my eyes. Enough was enough. We'd been sitting around this empty classroom for almost twenty minutes—and we hadn't accomplished anything. And I had to leave to get to my volleyball game. I held up the list of articles for our next 'zine and shook it. "You guys, could we get back to—"

"I know exactly what I did wrong," Brian announced, ignoring me. He ripped another piece of paper out of his notebook and started folding it. "Wider wings."

Oh, brother. I let the paper drop back down on the desk and rested my head on my hands. I love my friends, but sometimes they drive me crazy. And this was important. We were meeting after school to decide on the articles for the next issue of *Zone,* the online magazine we'd created for our school.

At the beginning of the year Brian, Salvador, Anna Wang, and I had all worked for the school paper, the *Spectator.* But we quit after a couple of weeks and decided to create our own magazine, where we could write the kinds of things *we* wanted to write.

Only now it looked like we weren't going to write anything.

Brian and Salvador were throwing paper airplanes, and even Anna was starting to get in on the action. They were like the Three Stooges . . . or a bunch of circus clowns—except for the fact that they don't look anything alike. Brian is tall and has blond hair; Salvador has dark, curly hair; and Anna is Asian-American. But they all have goofy smiles. Especially when they're together. I was ready to strangle them all. They *knew* I was in a hurry to make it to the gym too.

"Come on, you guys," I pleaded. "We still

need to think of one more article. Can we try to be constructive?"

Salvador smiled at me, his black eyes twinkling. "I am being constructive. I'm constructing paper airplanes."

I groaned. Brian and Anna laughed.

Suddenly Salvador slapped a palm to his forehead. "I've got it. Let's do a fashion review of the teachers."

Brian grinned. "Great idea. Ms. Upton's been wearing the same black shoes since before we were born."

"And what about that icky old fish tie Mr. Martinez wears every Friday?" Anna added. Her nose wrinkled. "What's up with that?"

I sighed, but I had to smile. "You guys are hopeless," I muttered. I glanced up at the clock. It was already almost a quarter to four. *Oh, well,* I thought. "We should probably just forget it," I said. "I've got to go anyway. The game starts in fifteen minutes, and I don't want to miss the warm-up." I shoved my notebook into my backpack and stood up. "Hey, why don't you guys come and watch? We could use somebody to cheer for us."

Anna shook her head. "Can't. Sorry. I've got a whole math chapter to finish before I even start on science."

"I can't either," Salvador chimed in. "The Doña is making me go to her kick-boxing class tonight."

"Your grandmother's into *kick boxing?*" Brian asked dubiously. "No way."

"Yes way." Salvador shrugged. "She decided tai chi wasn't strenuous enough for her."

"Brian?" I asked. I raised my eyebrows hopefully. "Do you want to come?"

He scratched his head for a minute, then nodded. "Sure." He flashed me a crooked grin. "Anything to avoid homework."

I was actually kind of surprised, but I didn't say anything as we packed up our stuff and headed to the gym. The fact of the matter is that almost *nobody* ever watches us play. And we needed all the support we could get. It's a miracle if the entire team even shows up for a game. Sweet Valley Junior High didn't even really *have* a team until a couple of weeks ago. Volleyball here is really laid-back—for a lot of different reasons.

The biggest of them all is Blue Spiccoli.

Speak of the devil, I thought as Brian and I opened the big double doors to the gym. There was Blue, standing apart from the rest of the team, absently batting a ball up and down. His brother, Leaf, was doing the same thing. And

Leaf is the *coach*. I couldn't help but smile. Both Blue and Leaf were wearing flip-flops and cutoff shorts. The rest of the team was wearing sneakers, of course—but I'm sure that wearing sneakers didn't even cross Blue's mind. The Spiccoli brothers think differently from most people. Being "mellow" is the most important thing in their lives.

"Hey, Blue!" I called.

His face lit up with a big grin the moment he saw me, and he grabbed the ball. My own smile widened. Blue has the most amazing blue eyes and bright, almost bleached blond hair. It's probably because he spends every spare minute of his life down at the beach, surfing.

"Hey," he said, walking up to Brian and me with the ball tucked under his arm. "What's shaking? Are you psyched to play?"

"Of course," I said. I nodded toward Brian. "Blue, this is my friend Brian. He volunteered to cheer us on."

Blue nodded appreciatively and extended a hand. "Right on, bro. Thanks a lot."

Brian flashed a quick glance at me out of the corner of his eye as he shook Blue's hand. I could tell he was a little surprised by the way Blue talked, as if Brian wasn't sure if he was supposed to take Blue seriously or not. But once you get used to Blue's lingo, you hardly even notice it. I think it's kind of cute too—in a weird way.

"You run track, right?" Blue asked.

"Uh-huh," Brian said.

"I thought I'd seen you out there." Blue looked over Brian and nodded thoughtfully. "You know, it would be rad if you joined the volleyball team. You'd be a great spiker. The taller you are, the easier it is to slam the ball down over the net."

Brian grinned. "Really? I think I could get into spiking."

"Here," Blue offered. "Give it a shot."

He took a few steps back, then tossed the volleyball high in the air. Without missing a beat, Brian jumped up and spiked the ball hard down on the floor: *smack!* A few heads turned toward us. Blue laughed and grabbed the ball as it came back down from a huge bounce. Then he raised his hand for a high five.

"Killer slam, bro!" he exclaimed. "You're a natural."

Brian laughed too, then slapped Blue's hand. "Thanks . . . bro," he said cheerfully. He gave me a little shrug, as if to say: *Why not?*

I smirked. I should have known those guys would get along. Both of them like to goof around. A lot.

Blue

By the time the game was over, I was majorly tired. Volleyball can take a lot out of you, especially if the other team is good. And San Mateo is, like, *amazing*. They beat us pretty badly. But whatever. I don't care much about winning or losing. Neither does the rest of the team. It's just fun to play. Wicked fun.

Especially with Elizabeth Wakefield.

I stood on the sidelines, wiping away the sweat and watching her as she climbed up the bleachers to talk to her friend Brian. I felt a weird little flip in my stomach . . . but in that good kind of way, like the way you feel when you're zooming down the face of a radical wave. Elizabeth's smile has that effect on me.

Did I mention that she has a killer smile?

"Earth to Blue," Leaf called. "Come in, Blue. We've lost all contact. . . ."

I turned and rolled my eyes. Leaf was snickering and rolling up the net, which meant we were going to go home soon. Usually, I dig

7

going home, because that's when the fun starts. Leaf and I live alone in this killer pad by the beach. It's just been the two of us ever since my parents died when I was really young. But I never let it bum me out. Leaf does an awesome job of taking care of me. He lets me live my own life, which is why I always associate home with good times.

But going home meant *not* hanging out with Elizabeth.

I stood there, watching her talk to Brian, wishing I could think of something else to say to her. I'm not a shy dude by nature. But it's not exactly easy to ask a girl to do stuff. Especially a girl like Elizabeth. I didn't have the guts to just come out and ask her to hang out. Besides, what would we do? She doesn't surf, or skateboard, or play video games—and I'm pretty sure I don't do . . . whatever it is she does when she's not at school.

Probably schoolwork, I thought. Elizabeth is really smart. And she's in like four zillion clubs. I think she actually likes all that school stuff. I wish I did. It would probably make my life a lot easier.

"Ready?" Leaf called.

I nodded, but I couldn't bring myself to turn away from her.

Suddenly I felt a slap on the back. It was my friend Rick. His blond hair was moist with sweat from the game. "So, Blue, dude—pizza at your house?"

"Sure," I said automatically. Everybody's always welcome at my house. But then an idea dawned on me. Elizabeth and I might not have much in common, but we both had to eat, right?

I turned back to the bleachers and cupped my hands around my mouth. "Hey, Liz," I called. "Why don't you and Brian come and have pizza with us?"

Brian nodded eagerly, but Elizabeth bit her lip. She glanced over at Leaf. "You sure it's all right?" she asked.

"Of course it's all right," Leaf answered for me as he stored the net in a big crate by the side of the court.

I shrugged and smiled. "See?" I said.

Elizabeth and Brian glanced at each other, then Elizabeth nodded—as if she was really stoked. My stomach did that little flip again. "I just gotta call my parents," she said.

"Me too," Brian added.

"No problem," I replied. "We'll meet you out front."

I kept smiling as I watched the two of them head for the phones out in the hall. For a second

9

I wondered if she and Brian were, like . . . a *thing*—but no, it didn't seem like they were. They were just buds. And that was cool with me.

". . . any new games?"

"Huh?" I jumped a little. I hadn't even realized Rick was talking to me.

His eyes narrowed, as if he was trying to figure out if there was something wrong with me. "I was just wondering if Leaf had designed any new games," he said.

"Oh." I shrugged. "Yeah. He's working on something called Desert Commandos. It's pretty cool."

Rick's face brightened. "Excellent."

I nodded. In addition to coaching volleyball and taking care of me, Leaf also designs video games for a living. How awesome is that? He doesn't really talk to me about money and stuff, but I think he made like a bazillion dollars from a game he designed when he was in college. All I know is, we've got plenty of money to do whatever we want.

It doesn't make up for losing my parents. But it doesn't hurt either.

"Hey, do you think we should give Jaimie a call when we get to your house and see if she wants to come over?" Rick asked.

I opened my mouth to say yes, then closed it.

Hmmm, I thought. Jaimie's an older girl who lives in our neighborhood. I've been friends with her forever. She's a radical surfer and has the most awesome blond dreadlocks. But she and Elizabeth had met once before, and Elizabeth wasn't exactly very friendly. It was when I showed up late to a volleyball game. Jaimie and Rick were with me because we'd gone surfing, and Elizabeth kind of freaked out on me for blowing off the team. She was right; I *should* have been there on time. And anyway, Elizabeth had mellowed a lot since then. Besides, it's impossible not to get along with Jaimie. She's wicked cool. There was nothing to worry about. Right?

"Blue?" Rick asked. "Is something wrong?"

I shook my head. "Not at all," I said. But I wasn't so sure.

Do not stress, I told myself. *Everybody is gonna get along great. Right?*

Kristin Seltzer's Carnival Committee Meeting To-Do List

1. Decide on final decorations at tomorrow's meeting—balloon rainbow arch for the entry or bunches of balloons and streamers?
2. Draw map of where all booths and games will go.
3. Make *sure* Pete Coulter's brother will actually show up with his karaoke machine.
4. Make Lacey promise she'll come to the carnival and not make fun of it.

Elizabeth

"You won't believe the video-game setup they have here, Brian," Rick was yelling at Brian over the roar of Leaf's beat-up old van. "They've got, like, every single game on the planet."

I was bouncing up and down in the middle seat, smiling at Blue, but we hadn't been able to do much talking because the engine was so loud. In a way, though, I was relieved. What *could* I talk about with Blue? Or his friends? Aside from volleyball, we didn't have a whole lot in common. Maybe I'd made a big mistake by coming here. I wondered if Brian was as uncomfortable as I was. *Nope,* I realized. He and Rick had been talking for the entire ride.

Before I knew it, the van pulled into the driveway of a tiny, white-and-green house right on the beach, then lurched to a stop.

"Here we are, gang," Leaf called. The engine finally sputtered into silence. "Everybody out."

Brian, Blue, and Rick immediately shoved

open the van doors and ran for the house. For a moment I just sat there in the silence. It seemed like Brian already fit in perfectly, like he'd already been here a hundred times. I took a deep breath. Mingling isn't one of my best skills. My twin sister, Jessica, rules in that department, but I've never been as smooth as she is.

Leaf glanced over his shoulder and smiled at me as he pulled the keys out of the ignition.

"What kind of pizza do you like?" he asked.

I shrugged. "Any kind, I guess. Whatever you guys want is fine with me."

Leaf shook his head. "No, no, no. The guests always get to choose. We want to make our visitors happy." He raised his eyebrows. "Of course, if you chose pepperoni, I don't think anyone would complain. . . ."

I started laughing, and so did Leaf. I began to feel much better. What was I worried about anyway? These guys were so easygoing. Leaf was going out of his way to make me feel at home. It would be impossible *not* to have fun.

"Pepperoni sounds great," I said as I climbed out of the van.

The Spiccolis' house was really cute and traditional on the outside—but on the inside, it was like nothing I'd ever seen. For one thing, it probably hadn't been cleaned in months. On the wall over the couch was a huge sailfish wearing a lei of plastic flowers with blinking Christmas lights and a goofy canvas hat. The coffee table was piled with old pizza boxes. None of the furniture matched. There were two crushed velvet easy chairs, brown and green, and the couch was sky blue. An inflatable hula-girl doll grinned crazily from a corner of the living room. Five surfboards stood against the wall. From the lumps of dirty wax on them, I guessed they were boards Leaf and Blue actually used.

Amazing. My mom would probably have a heart attack if she saw this place.

Brian, Rick, and Blue were already huddled around a computer at the far end of the living room, staring intently at a screen filled with little green army men. I sighed. Video games weren't something that particularly interested me, but I supposed I could give it a shot. I'd never really played before, except at a few friends' birthdays.

Blue glanced over his shoulder. "Come here, Liz. There's a game I want you to try. It's called Wonder Woman. You know, like that old show with that woman who does all the lipstick commercials?"

I smiled and nodded as if I knew what he was talking about, then tentatively approached. The truth is, I can usually understand only about half

15

of what Blue says. Leaf appeared from behind me with a huge stuffed beanbag, then tossed it on the floor so I would have a place to sit.

The three guys made room for me in front of the computer. Blue handed me a joystick. I could feel my face getting hot as I settled into the beanbag. *This won't take very long,* I thought. I'd probably be killed or blown up or eaten or whatever happens in a video game in a matter of seconds. Bells and wild, high-pitched noises blared from the screen. The living room sounded like an arcade.

"Now, the object is to escape the burning factory and kill all the bad guys," Rick instructed. "There are a couple of tricky parts—"

The doorbell rang. I breathed a secret sigh of relief. Maybe this would provide me with an excuse not to play. Leaf ran to get it. An older girl with long, blond dreadlocks stepped into the house. She looked like she was about seventeen or eighteen. And she was *very* familiar.

"Hey, Jaimie," Blue and Leaf said at the same time.

"What's up, guys?" she said.

My eyes narrowed. I'd definitely seen this girl before. . . .

"Hey, I remember you!" Jaimie said, smiling at me. "You're on the volleyball team."

16

All at once my face reddened. *That's* where I'd seen her before. In the gym, at the very first game I'd ever played. She was with Rick and Blue when they'd arrived late and I'd thrown a tantrum. *Uh-oh,* I thought. *This could get ugly.*

"You have a wicked serve," she said approvingly.

"Uh . . . thanks," I mumbled, trying to smile back. I couldn't believe how polite she was being after the way I'd acted.

"Jaimie, this is Liz and Brian," Blue cut in, waving his hands at us.

Rick tapped me on the shoulder. "Hey, Liz—don't you want to play this game?"

I glanced between him and Jaimie. "Uh . . ."

Jaimie put her hands on her hips and smirked, pretending to be upset. "It's a beautiful night out, and you're forcing this poor girl to play video games? Where are your manners, dudes?" She winked at me and waved me to the door. "Come on. I want to show you something."

"Really?" I asked.

She nodded. "The sunset's amazing from here. It goes down right over the water, and there are all these different colors. It's really intense."

"Cool," I found myself saying—relieved to have an excuse *not* to humiliate myself at the computer. I handed the joystick to Blue and hopped up from the beanbag.

Blue's brow was furrowed. "But don't you want to be Wonder Woman?" he asked softly.

"I think sunsets are more my speed," I answered with a laugh.

"Uh . . . okay," he said reluctantly. "But you have to promise you'll give it a try at some point."

I nodded. "Definitely." I almost felt like adding: *I'm willing to try anything.* Everybody here was such a free spirit. Video games, sunsets, pizza . . . and all on a school night. What could be better?

Blue

"Die, supervillains!" Rick yelled.

He and Brian were cracking up as they played Desert Commandos. Rick raised his arms and wiggled his fingers as if he was getting ready to conduct an orchestra or something. Then he started pounding the joystick button furiously.

"Way to go!" Brian yelled.

I shook my head. Normally I would have been hooting and hollering too. But I was starting to get bummed. I couldn't even pay attention to the action on-screen—and this was one of my brother's coolest games. This was totally *not* going the way I had planned it. Elizabeth was supposed to be in here with me. Not checking out the sunset with Jaimie on the porch.

So go out there and join them, I said to myself.

I smiled. Yeah. I *could* join them. Why not?

"Hey, where are you going, dude?" Rick called as I headed for the door.

"I just want to see if the pizza guy's here

19

yet," I lied. I didn't want Rick or Brian to think that I was hung up on Elizabeth or anything. I wasn't. Not really. I just wanted to get to know her better.

A cool evening breeze hit me as I stepped out onto the porch. Man, I love living by the water. I can't imagine living anywhere else. I could hear the waves crashing, and around the corner Jaimie and Elizabeth laughing together. *Good,* I thought. It was cool that Elizabeth was getting along so well with my friends.

I rounded the corner to the side of the house that faced the beach. The sun had just sunk below the horizon, and the sky was a really intense red. Both girls were leaning over the railing, staring out at the ocean.

"What's up, guys?" I asked.

Elizabeth shook her head and smiled at me, wide-eyed. "Wow," she said. "You're so lucky. You get to see a sunset like this every day."

I shrugged, trying not to stare at her. But she has the cutest face, with these sky blue eyes and a little nose. I loved how she didn't seem to have a clue about how pretty she was. Most girls at our school would be all snotty about it.

"I know," I said finally. Watching the sunset is actually one of my favorite things to do—ever since I was little. "The best is when—"

"Hey, I think the pizza guy's here!" Jaimie suddenly exclaimed.

I turned around. Sure enough, I heard the sound of a car door slamming, then footsteps coming up the front stairs.

"Man, am I hungry," Jaimie commented. She hurried around the corner.

I turned to Elizabeth, hoping that we could enjoy a little time alone together, but she was right on Jaimie's heels.

"Me too," she was saying. "I could eat a whole pizza myself!"

My shoulders sagged. I hadn't acted fast enough. But what would I have said to her anyway? *I think you're really cute and awesome.* Yeah, right. I probably just would have put my foot in my mouth and said something even more lame than that. Still, I hadn't even gotten a chance to *try* to say something.

It was cool that Elizabeth was getting along with my friends so well . . . but what about *me*?

Brian

"I don't think I can move." I groaned.

Everybody in the room laughed—but their faces were pained. We'd split five pizzas six ways, and those last two slices had definitely been two too many. Nobody could even muster the energy to play with the computer anymore. We were all sprawled on the couch and easy chairs, with pizza boxes and crusts and empty soda cans everywhere. Well, except Leaf. He had just decided to stretch out on the rug beside the coffee table. I couldn't help but wonder what my parents would think if they walked into this room. They'd probably scream. Especially when they saw Leaf's tattoos.

"Hey, we never got Liz to play any games," Leaf suddenly remarked.

Elizabeth just shook her head. She was slouched in the couch next to Jaimie with her eyes closed and her hands over her stomach. "I'm too wiped out," she murmured. "Besides, I don't know if killing supervillains with a machine gun is up my alley."

Leaf sat up straight. "I'm actually thinking about a new game where the characters are wizards," he said. "It would be more of a fantasy kind of thing. You know, castle mazes, enchanted forests. What do you think? Would you play that?"

"Actually, that sounds neat," Elizabeth said. She opened her eyes and smiled. "I'm just not into the whole bloodshed thing."

Suddenly I had an idea. "Hey, what if the players had magic wands instead of weapons?" I suggested. "That way there wouldn't have to be any blood at all."

Leaf's eyes bulged. He clapped. "Oh, wow, dude!" he exclaimed. "Rad idea! That rules!"

"You think?" I shrugged, trying to act like it was no big deal. Inside, I was doing a back flip. I could not believe I was having this conversation. Leaf thought *my* idea was great? He was, like . . . a *genius*.

"Hey, we should probably go into the bedroom," Blue said. "I saw in *TV Guide* that *Terminator 2* is on at eight. I've never seen it before."

Jaimie bolted upright. "Really?" she exclaimed, looking shocked. "I can't *believe* that, dude. You're gonna love it. It's so awesome."

What I can't believe is that Blue has a T.V. in his bedroom and gets to hang out and have pizza parties on a school night, I thought.

I was a little jealous of Blue. I had no idea he had such a great life. I mean, the guy lives at the beach and surfs every day, and his house is full of experimental video games. *And* he gets to live with Leaf—who lets him do whatever he wants. I wished that my older brother was like Leaf. But Billy is about as different from Leaf as a person can get. He's a total jock. He thinks volleyball and surfing are for wimps.

All at once Elizabeth bolted upright. She stared at Blue. Her brow was tightly furrowed. "Wait a second," she said. "Did you say that we should move now to catch a movie that starts at *eight?*"

"Yeah." Blue casually pointed at a small digital clock next to the computer. "It starts in five minutes."

Uh-oh. My stomach dropped. I met Elizabeth's gaze. I knew that she was thinking the exact same thing as I was. We'd completely lost track of the time. We should have called our parents almost an hour ago.

"I gotta go," I muttered, forcing myself to stand. "My parents are gonna *kill* me."

"Mine too," Elizabeth mumbled.

We nearly bumped into each other as we hopped up and searched the living room for a phone. But the place was so messy. All I could see were the remnants of our meal. My stomach heaved queasily. How could I have forgotten to call my parents? No, the question was: How could Elizabeth have forgotten to call *hers?* She's the most responsible person I know.

"Lookin' for a phone, bro?" Blue asked. He reached under a throw pillow and pulled out a cordless phone, then tossed it to me.

I snatched it out of the air and hurriedly punched in my number. My palms were a little moist. If there is one thing my parents hate, it's not knowing where I am or what I'm doing. They're sort of controlling that way.

After only one ring somebody picked up. "Hello?"

I swallowed hard. It was Mom. She sounded anxious.

"Um . . . hi," I said tentatively.

"Brian!" She yelled so loud, I had to pull the phone away from my ear. "Where are you? We've been worried to death."

I glanced around the living room. I guess everyone else could hear her too. Elizabeth bit her lip. Jaimie winced. Rick, Blue, and Leaf just stared sheepishly down at the floor.

"We're still at Blue's house," I explained, trying to sound as apologetic as I could. "We sort of forgot about the time. I'm really, really sorry—"

"Hello?" Somebody else picked up the phone. I rolled my eyes. It was Billy.

"I've got it, Billy," my mother said.

"Who is it?" he asked.

"It's Brian," she replied.

I glanced around the living room again. This was getting more embarrassing by the second. I felt like I was on display or something. I knew my face must be bright red.

"Brian?" Billy demanded. "Where are you?"

"Uh . . . I'm still at Blue's," I mumbled as quietly as I could.

"Blue *Spiccoli?*" Billy cried. He let out a harsh little laugh. "What are you doing over there? That guy's a total space cadet. He lives with his brother in some dump by the beach and—"

"We'll talk about it later," Mom growled, cutting him off. "I'm in the middle of making dinner, so I'm sending Billy to pick you up." She paused. "He might as well give Elizabeth a ride home too. I'm sure her parents would appreciate it."

"Hey!" Billy protested. "Don't I—"

"Bye," I said, pressing the button to hang up. I sighed miserably. My heart was pounding. But in spite of my mom's anger, I wasn't even so worried about how much trouble I was going to be in when I got home. No, mostly I was mad at Billy. Why did he have to say those things about Blue? They weren't even true. Billy had no idea what he was talking about. Blue was *not* a space cadet, and his house was *not* a dump. In fact, it was just about the coolest house I'd ever seen.

I glanced at Elizabeth, shaking my head. "Billy'll be here in a few minutes to get us," I grumbled. "He'll give you a ride."

She nodded. Her face was kind of pale. "Thanks." She took the phone from me. "I guess I better call my parents too."

Leaf gave me a reassuring smile. "Everything okay?"

I ran my fingers through my hair and shrugged. "Well . . . not quite," I said. I forced a laugh—even though I felt sick.

Not even close, I added silently.

Note from Jessica Wakefield to Elizabeth Wakefield

Liz—

I borrowed your pink hair scrunchie. Hope that's okay.

I'm studying at the library with Bethel.

See you tonight.

PS: Mom and Dad are really mad!

E-mail from Bethel McCoy to Kristin Seltzer

To: KGgrl99
From: Runfast
Re: Carnival idea

Kristin—

Ms. Kern wanted me to tell you that she called the rental company, and we are definitely getting the sumo wrestling, the Velcro wall jumping, and the human-darts game set up.

I was thinking, if there's not enough room in the gym, what if we skip the ring toss and keep the smash-a-bug instead? I think the guys would go for that more. Just a suggestion.

—Bethel

Kristin

I hurried through the hall to my locker on Wednesday morning, trying to decide if the funny feeling in my stomach was stress or excitement. I figured it was both. There were only three more days until the carnival. *Three.* After all those weeks of work it was finally going to happen. The biggest carnival SVJH had ever had! I'd been imagining it in my mind for so long, I couldn't wait to see the gym decorated and packed with kids.

The planning hadn't exactly gone smoothly either. Bethel McCoy and I nearly killed each other over the details. But once we learned how to compromise, we finally worked everything out. And now I was confident. *Supremely* confident. I tossed my blond curls over my shoulder and grinned. It was going to be—

"Hey, Kristin! Slow down!"

I stopped in my tracks and laughed. I'd been so preoccupied that I hadn't even noticed Brian, who was just closing the locker he shares with

Elizabeth. And Brian's a hard guy not to notice. Especially because he's so good-looking. *Especially* because he's my boyfriend. Am I lucky or what?

"What's the hurry?" he asked with a puzzled grin.

"Nothing," I said breathlessly. "Guess what? All the prizes just got delivered to Ms. Kern's room, and the little blue bears are even cuter than I thought they'd be." I knew I was talking at the speed of light, but I was having a hard time keeping all my thoughts straight. The carnival was all-consuming. There was so much to do before Saturday. "The cotton-candy machine is getting delivered later."

He shrugged and slung his knapsack over his arm. His grin faded. "That's nice," he mumbled.

I clutched his arm. "You promised to help me out this week, right? There's going to be a lot of stuff to do at the last minute. We're getting a Slushie machine too, and we need to figure out the flavors."

"Uh . . . yeah. Right." He stared down at the floor, then laughed grimly. "I'll help you with everything. If my parents ever let me out of the house again."

My hand fell to my side. "What do you mean?" I asked, confused.

He shook his head and rolled his eyes. "My

parents are mad at me for the dumbest reason. I went over to Blue Spiccoli's house last night with Liz, and we just kind of lost track of the time—"

"Whoa, whoa . . . wait a second," I interrupted, holding up my hands. Now I was totally baffled. "What were you doing over at Blue Spiccoli's house?"

Brian shrugged. "He invited me there," he replied simply.

My eyes narrowed. There had to be something he wasn't telling me. Blue Spiccoli hardly even comes to *school*, much less invites random strangers to his house. As far as I know, he spends all his time surfing. He doesn't even live with his parents. That's what the rumor is anyway.

"What?" Brian asked in the silence. He grinned.

I shook my head. "I . . . um—I just didn't know you knew him," I stammered awkwardly. I didn't want to make it seem like going to Blue's was a bad thing to do. Of course, I didn't necessarily think it was a *good* thing, but . . .

"Hey, guys!" Elizabeth called through the crowd in the hall. She snaked her way over to the locker and began turning the combination lock. "How's it going?"

I shrugged. To be honest, I was so confused

at the moment, I couldn't even answer her.

"Wasn't that fun last night?" Brian asked Elizabeth.

Elizabeth laughed. The locker door popped open. "Yeah. Everything except the coming-home part."

Brian nodded sympathetically. "Tell me about it," he said with a moan.

"Are you in trouble?" she asked in a hushed voice.

"No. My mom had calmed down by the time I got home. You?"

Elizabeth shook her head, grabbed a few books, then closed the locker. "They're mad, but I'm not grounded or anything."

They grinned at each other. Both of them had this excited glimmer in their eyes, as if they were sharing a secret. As if they'd done something really special. Together. Without me. How did they even end up at Blue Spiccoli's house anyway? Neither of them surf. At least, not as far as I know.

"Hey, is everything going okay with the carnival?" Elizabeth asked me.

"Huh?" I asked. For a second I'd forgotten all about the carnival. "Oh. Yeah. Sure."

She smiled. "I can't wait. Jessica says it's going to be so cool. Well, I gotta go. See you guys."

She shot Brian another quick glance, then took off down the hall.

I sighed. "So, anyway, speaking of the carnival, there's just one more thing—"

"I wonder if you could get Leaf to come down to give a video-game demonstration!" Brian interrupted excitedly.

Leaf? I stared at him, frowning. "Who's that?"

"He's Blue's brother. You know, that guy with tattoos who coaches volleyball? Anyway, he designs all these video games. You should see the stuff they've got in their house. And he's so incredibly cool. I'm sure he'd be up for it."

I stood there, staring at Brian as he jabbered on and on about Blue Spiccoli's completely fantastic and amazing brother. Had I entered some kind of bizarro alternate universe? I didn't *care* about Flower, or Plant, or whatever his name was. The conversation didn't even seem *real*.

". . . He even liked my idea about using a magic wand instead of a machine gun—"

"Um, Brian?" I interrupted flatly. "We already have enough stuff for the carnival. We don't need Blue Spiccoli's brother to do anything for it."

He blinked. "Oh." He smiled sheepishly. "Sorry. I guess I just got a little carried away. It really was fun, though. I wish you'd been there."

"Really?" I asked. And an amazing thing happened. At that moment, with the way he was staring at me with those big, bright eyes . . . I just forgot about my anger. It was silly anyway. I let out a huge breath. So he went to one party at Blue's house—so what? It wasn't like he was going to dump me because of it.

Sometimes I need to just relax. *Things will be better after the carnival,* I promised myself. Who knew? Maybe even *I'd* end up going to Blue Spiccoli's house.

Bethel

"Excuse me. Pardon me," I called out as I sprinted down the hall. I got a couple of funny looks as I dodged between knots of people at top speed, but hey, I was in a hurry. The band I'd used to pull my hair back into a ponytail had broken during second period, and my hair was falling in my face, driving me crazy. I had about ten seconds to duck into the girls' bathroom to fix it before third period started.

Finally I made it. I threw open the heavy wooden door and doubled over to catch my breath.

The first thing I saw was legs. Legs in black tights, with black combat boots and a short, black skirt. I looked up to see a familiar sneer.

Lacey Frells.

I took a quick look around and sighed. Nobody else was in the bathroom but her and me. It figured. It was one of those days where everything seems to go wrong. There's no one at SVJH I'd rather see less. Actually, there's no one on the *planet* I'd rather see less.

She glared at me.

Right back at ya, I thought. Then I strolled calmly to the mirror and dug into my backpack for a barrette to pull back my hair. Lacey's snobbishness is not worth getting upset about. I'd learned *that* a long time ago.

She headed for a stall. *Good,* I thought as I snapped a pink barrette in place. *Now I can pretend she isn't even here.*

"Oh no!"

I frowned, glancing over my shoulder. A strange, muted choking sound was coming from Lacey's stall.

"Oh no!" she cried again. "Oh . . . This isn't . . . What am I supposed to do now?"

Drown? I answered silently, chuckling to myself. She probably had a run in her tights or something. I slung my backpack over my shoulder and headed to the door—then paused. The toilet-paper dispenser in Lacey's stall was rattling like she was pulling off a zillion yards of the stuff.

"This is *so* not okay," she muttered. Her voice was fast and breathless. "This is so bad. This is so bad."

I froze, listening. Was she actually in some kind of trouble?

She went on mumbling to herself, but I couldn't make out the words. Still, she not only sounded unhappy, she sounded *scared*.

"What am I going to *do?*" she asked again.

My hands tightened on the straps of my backpack. Maybe I should . . . should what? Offer to help? Help Lacey Frells? Was I stupid? I took another step toward the door. But I just couldn't go any farther. I sighed loudly and rolled my eyes. I knew I was going to regret this.

"Is something wrong?" I asked.

"No," she snapped.

Yup. What had I expected? "Good," I shot back. "See you later."

"Bethel, wait," she called out.

Coming from Lacey, it sounded more like a command than a request. I crossed my arms over my chest and tapped my foot on the floor. "*What?*" I demanded.

"I—I need . . ." Her voice trailed off. She cleared her throat. I heard the sound of the bell ringing through the door. Great. Now I was officially late.

"I'm in kind of a hurry, Lacey," I stated.

"I mean, do you have anything for . . . *you*

know," she choked out. "I think I just started . . . and I . . ."

All of a sudden it dawned on me. *Duh,* I thought. Only one scenario could possibly be so embarrassing that it would force a jerk like Lacey Frells to beg somebody she hated for help.

"Did you need a pad?" I asked.

There was a second of silence. "I guess," she finally mumbled.

"You're having your period, right?"

"Would I be stuck in here if I wasn't?" she shrieked.

I frowned. Something else occurred to me too. Judging from the way she was freaking out, this might be her very *first* period. I swallowed. Now I actually felt kind of bad. I let my backpack slide off my shoulder. "Wow. Okay. I guess—"

"So do you have any, you know, stuff or what?" she spat out from behind the stall door.

I opened my mouth to say something mean back, but I just couldn't. The truth is, I *did* feel sorry for her. I know, I know. How could I have any sympathy whatsoever for the queen brat of SVJH? Still, nobody—not even Lacey—deserved to get her first period at school, alone in the bathroom with an enemy. I remember how freaked *I* was when it happened. And I was lucky. It was over the summer, and I was even at home. My mom got all the right things for me and talked me through it.

"Yeah, I've got some stuff," I said. I bent down and unzipped my backpack, then fished a pad out of the little bag I kept in the bottom. "This is what you need," I told her as I slipped the pad under the stall door. "It'll last you through the end of the day."

"Okay," she barked. Her fingers snatched it up. "I don't need a lecture."

I crouched there for a minute, unable to believe her response. I wasn't sure if I wanted to laugh or give her door a good, swift kick. No "thanks," no "I really appreciate this, Bethel"—just "okay." But what did I expect? That was Lacey. Rude. Ungrateful. Bratty. Embarrassing things happen to bad people too. Being humiliated doesn't turn you into a saint.

"You're welcome," I snapped. I picked up my knapsack and stormed out of the bathroom.

"Hey, Bethel—"

But the door slammed shut behind me, cutting her off. I didn't really care either. She was on her own. I'd helped her plenty.

Brian

"Okay, guys, here's the schedule for the rest of the week."

I tried to listen to Kristin, but it was kind of hard. The carnival committee was meeting during lunch in Ms. Kern's room. *Again.* When would I be able to eat in the cafeteria, like a normal person? Plan, plan, plan. It seemed like that was all we ever did anymore.

"We've got a lot of ground to cover, so pay attention," Kristin was saying.

I squinted down at my paper. *No good,* I thought, frowning. I was trying to draw a post-nuclear mutant, but it looked more like a raspberry with feet than a monster. I sighed and crossed it out. Ever since I'd been to the Spiccolis' house, I'd been obsessed with drawing new ideas for Leaf to use in his work. Not that I honestly believed he *would* actually use any of them, of course. But still, it was fun. And way harder than I thought it would be.

"Tomorrow we're meeting at the mall, right in

41

front of the party store," Kristin announced. "And of course Friday's going to be superbusy."

I turned my paper sideways, studying the mutant's eyes. *Not mean enough,* I decided. Maybe heavier eyebrows.

Kristin was still talking. "We'll meet at lunch to go over final assignments for Saturday, then everybody'll have their individual jobs Friday after school. Now, I'll read off your jobs."

Boy, she was starting to sound stressed. Kristin's normally really cheerful. This carnival thing was wearing her down. I was glad it was going to be over soon.

"Brian?"

I looked up. She was staring right at me, a big frown on her face.

Whoops. I covered up my drawing with my hand and sat up straight, trying to smile as if I'd been paying attention the whole time.

Kristin cleared her throat. "You all should probably write down the details of your assignment, don't you think?"

"Oh yeah," I said. "Yeah." I bent my head over my paper and drew prickly hairs on the mutant's chin. She didn't have to know that I wasn't taking notes. I already knew my jobs for the week. No way I'd forget. Kristin would kill me.

Blue

Wednesday, I couldn't wait to get home after school. The surf had been totally awesome in the morning when I left, and I was hoping Leaf would catch a few waves with me before dinner. It was a perfect day for it—windy and not a cloud in the sky.

"Hey, Leaf," I yelled as soon as I opened the front door. "You wanna hit the beach?"

"Come here, Blue," he called.

Hmmm. I swallowed, not liking the sound of his voice. It was stern and harsh and totally stressed out. And when I saw him in the living room, I didn't feel any better. He was sitting on the couch with the cordless phone on his knee, staring into space. The computer wasn't on. Neither was the stereo. Or the TV. In our house *something* is usually on. The silence was a little eerie.

I sat down on the arm of the couch without even bothering to take off my knapsack. "What's up?" I asked.

Leaf leaned back a little. He didn't even look at me. His jaw was tightly set. "Social services just called," he stated. "We've got a new social worker, and she decided to check up on you. She talked to the school." He turned and looked me right in the eye. "Your grades are bombing big time, Blue."

At first I couldn't even process everything he'd said. We'd gotten a new social worker? How come nobody told us? I swallowed again, hard, and stared down at my shoes. There was nothing I could say either. My grades *did* stink. I'd been blowing off schoolwork for weeks. It's not like I hate it or anything. Sometimes, though, I just can't get into it. Leaf always tells me that he's there to help, but I don't like to bug him about stuff. He's got enough on his mind as it is. And he never gets on my case about it. Not usually anyway.

"Something's gotta change, Blue," he added.

Now my heart started beating a little faster. I hadn't thought about social services in a long time. I'd forgotten about the power that they have. Leaf is my legal guardian, but child welfare has the right to check up on us and make sure I'm in an okay environment. And if they don't like what they see . . . well, I didn't even want to think about that.

"So what did she say, exactly?" I asked in the silence.

Leaf raised his eyebrows. "She wasn't happy. Your grades have slipped from Bs to Ds. And it sounds like a couple of your teachers complained that you don't seem to pay much attention in class. And the principal's worried because you don't participate in extracurricular things either."

I shook my head. There had to be something I could say in my defense—but what? "What about volleyball?" I countered.

"Yeah, volleyball counts," Leaf said with a shrug. But he didn't sound very convinced. "You can explain that to the social worker when she comes this weekend."

My eyes bulged. I nearly fell off the couch. "She—She's coming here this weekend?" I stammered.

"Uh-huh." He nodded grimly. "But I don't know what day or time. It's a surprise visit."

"No." I shook my head. "No. Not this weekend. It's not enough time."

Leaf blinked a few times. He opened his mouth, then closed it. His shoulders seemed to sag a little bit. "It'll be all right," he murmured after a while. "We've always passed inspection before."

45

Something in his voice seemed to add: *But we won't this time.* I stood up. My knees were wobbly. A terrible thought popped into my brain. I stared at my brother. "What if they blame you for my grades? They're gonna say you're a bad parent, that you don't supervise me enough. What if—" I had to stop. A lump was growing in my throat. I could feel myself starting to panic. "What if they take me away?" I whispered. "What if they want to put me in a foster home?"

"They're not going to do that," he stated.

I shook my head. If he was so certain of that, he wouldn't have mentioned my lousy grades in the first place.

"Blue, hey—look at me." His green eyes bored right into mine. "It's going to be okay. I promise. We're family. No one is going to take you away from me. Okay?"

"Okay," I whispered. My voice was strained.

We didn't say anything for a minute. But I knew there was nothing *to* say. The fact of the matter was that somebody could take me away at any time. So I needed to prove to this new social worker that I was just fine living with my brother.

I had to get my life in gear. Fast.

Blue Spiccoli's Wednesday To-Do List

1. Make to-do list. ✔
2. Call friends in English, math, and science. Find out what the homework has been for the last three weeks.
3. *Do not* panic.
4. Make list of books to bring home from school tomorrow.
5. Read the SVJH *Guide to Successful Studying*.
6. *Do not* fall asleep in class.
7. *Do not* get bored and log onto Surfwatcher Web site and check wave conditions for this weekend.
8. Read instructions for clock radio.
9. Set alarm for ~~7 A.M.~~ ~~6:45~~. Okay, 6:30.

Lacey

Is it possible to die from cramps?

I couldn't run. I could barely *move*. I felt like I weighed twice as much as I usually did. I was in a huge hurry to get home after school and call Kristin. But the pain was so bad, it took me forever just to walk up to the front door. I only hoped nobody was watching me. I looked like an old woman, all stiff and hunched over.

Actually, the question wasn't: *Can I die from cramps?* No, the question was: *Can I die from humiliation?*

I opened the door, dropped my backpack by the stairs, and leaned back against the wall. Ouch! Another wave of cramps hit. I squeezed my eyes shut and wrapped my arms tightly around my stomach, groaning. It wasn't even so much because of the agony. Nope. I was sure that snot Bethel had told the whole school by now. Now everyone would know that I was the last person in the world to start her period.

"Lacey!" Penelope, my half sister, yelled happily. "See my picture?"

My eyes shot open.

Penelope was sitting on the rug in front of the coffee table, coloring. Even worse, Victoria, my witch of a stepmother, was staring at me from the couch. She must have come home early from work. Great. I was having the worst day of my life, and now I had to deal with my evil stepmother. Sometimes it really stinks to be me.

"Hello, Lacey," Victoria said coolly. She was lying with her feet up on a pile of throw pillows. Victoria has been planted on that black leather couch ever since she announced she was pregnant. Too bad the couch was still in our house.

"Hi," I mumbled.

She brushed a perfectly manicured hand over her perfectly in-place hair. Her eyes flickered over my black boots and my short, black miniskirt. Then her lips twisted, as if she'd just sucked on a lemon. "Lacey, didn't we talk about appropriate school clothing last week?" she asked.

"*You* talked," I shot back. "I couldn't get a word in." I snatched up my backpack and stomped up the stairs. We'd had this conversation only a zillion times. Victoria doesn't like the way I dress. Which is fine. The feeling's mutual. In fact, there's absolutely *nothing* about her that I like. And there's absolutely no way I'd ever tell her about getting my period. I ran to my room and slammed the door behind me.

For a minute I stared at the phone on my desk. But then I flopped down on my unmade bed. I couldn't make myself dial Kristin's number. How humiliated was I going to be when my best friend found out I just started my period? Kristin thought I'd been having my period since sixth grade. I hadn't lied to her about it. Not exactly. It was just that when she started hers, she assumed I'd already had mine. And I didn't bother to correct her. No way I was going to look like a baby. Even if she *is* my best friend.

But what if she already knew?

I closed my eyes. Of course she knew. Bethel had already blabbed about it. Why wouldn't she? *I* definitely would have. I curled up into a little ball, with my knees drawn up to my chest. It was funny: I'd been dying to get my period since fifth grade. Actually, it wasn't so funny. How stupid was I?

After what seemed like hours the pain began to subside a little. I rolled over and reached for the phone, then dialed Kristin's number. It was better just to get this over with. She would tell me that the whole school now knew that I was a loser, and that would be that. On the plus side, I couldn't sink any lower.

After two rings Kristin answered. "Hello?" she said in her perky voice.

"Hey." I moaned.

"Oh—hey! What's up?" She sounded like nothing was wrong.

"Nothing," I said suspiciously. "I just thought I'd see what's up with you."

"I am *so* excited," she replied. "The Velcro wall-jumping game came after lunch today, and the janitors are setting it up. It looks so fun! A bunch of us stopped by the gym to see it. It was Bethel's idea, and at first I thought it would be lame, but— "

"Was Bethel there?" I asked, cutting her off.

There was a pause. "Well, yeah," Kristin answered hesitantly. "Like I said, it was her idea. Besides, she's on the carnival committee."

I chewed my lip. Was it possible that Kristin didn't even know about my . . . incident? No way. She must be avoiding the subject because she knew it would make me uncomfortable.

". . . and we're even having video recording for the karaoke machine so people can make music videos," she was saying.

My stomach knotted with cramps. I moaned out loud. I couldn't help it.

"Lacey, are you okay?"

"Just cramps," I managed to say through gritted teeth.

"Really?" she said nonchalantly. "I thought you never got them."

My eyes widened. Kristin didn't know! For a

51

moment I almost smiled. Bethel must not have told her. Kristin's no good at hiding things. But why did Bethel keep it a secret? Oh, well. There was no point in dwelling on it.

"Yeah, um, well, I never got cramps before," I said, trying to sound completely casual. "Weird, huh? So what do you take for them anyway?"

She hesitated. "Usually just ibuprofen. That's what my mom buys me. Ask Victoria to get you some."

Not. I wouldn't ask *her* for anything. But I could ask Dad and tell him that I had a headache. "Good idea," I said. "Look, I better go."

"Lace, promise me you'll come to the carnival, okay?" Kristin blurted out.

Now I really *did* smile. She thought I was acting weird because I didn't want to go to the carnival. "I'll think about it," I said.

"Okay," she murmured disappointedly. "Bye."

"Bye, Kristin."

I hung up and took a few deep breaths. First order of business: I had to talk to Dad about painkillers. Also, I was going to need some more products. But how was I going to manage that? Dad would probably pass out. Or worse, he'd make himself a martini and force me to talk it over with Victoria.

Well, it was no big deal. I'd just have to figure something out and make a plan on my own. Like always.

Wednesday Night

8:04 P.M. Kristin's halfway done with her algebra homework when she stops for the fifth time to obsess over the to-do lists for the carnival. She shuffles through the five scraps of paper with lists on them and realizes she's lost the list of refreshments. She pushes aside her algebra book. Refreshments are *way* more important.

8:07 P.M. Brian takes a break from his algebra homework after one problem and instead draws a series of giant reptiles for a video game idea he's working on.

8:56 P.M. Kristin can't see her floor because it's covered with everything that used to be on or in her desk. She still hasn't found the list of refreshments.

9:27 P.M. Brian opens his math book again and almost finishes another problem. But his *PC Gamer* magazine catches his eye. He thumbs through the whole issue, then, after chewing on the end of his pencil, erases the head on his reptile and draws three more.

9:38 P.M. Kristin leaves her destroyed room and searches every counter and tabletop in the house. Still no list. She sits on the floor in the living room and goes through her mother's stack of fashion and fitness magazines, just in case the list got stuck in one. No list.

10:24 P.M. Brian looks up from his sketches, sees the time, and remembers that he never finished his math homework. No problem. He'll get it from Kristin in the morning.

10:43 P.M. Kristin lies on the floor of her mother's car with a flashlight. She finds the refreshment list under the passenger seat and heads back to her room to finish her algebra. Only she's way too exhausted. No problem. She'll get it from Brian in the morning.

E-mails between Anna, Elizabeth, and Salvador

From: BigS1
To: wkfldE, ANA3
Re: My great article

Hey, guys—
   I attached my *Zone* article on why school uniforms are a dumb idea. What about a title? I have *no idea!!!*
                  —Sal

From: ANA3
To: wkfldE, BigS1
Re: My great article

   Okay, here are some of the ideas.
   "Give Me Freedom of Clothes or Give Me Death"
   "Don't Make Us Dress Like Dorks"
   "School Uniforms: A Stupid Idea"
   "Robotic Dressing? It Won't Work"
   "Clothes Don't Make the Student"
   Sorry I don't have any better ones right now, but I have to finish this English assignment. Yuck.
               XXXOOO, Anna

From: wkfldE
To: BigS1, ANA3
Re: My great article

Hi, you two—
   Salvador—I really like your article! I think we should put it on the front page. Here are my title ideas:

1. "Uniforms: What Would They Really Do?"
2. "We're *Not* Alike—Why Should We Dress That Way?"

By the way, I was thinking about maybe buying a skateboard. What do you guys think?

Love, Liz

Blue

I couldn't believe it.

Even at seven o'clock in the morning, kids were already hurrying through the halls. *Seven o'clock.* I had no clue so many people actually got to school that early. Didn't they sleep? I could barely keep my eyes open. I watched blearily as this little guy with a plaid shirt buttoned all the way to the top went into one of the math rooms. I followed him. Math's not exactly my favorite topic, but I was desperate. I *had* to impress that social worker. That meant scoring as many club memberships as possible.

There were about ten kids in the room. They all looked wide awake. I stood by the door, unsure if I should sit with them or not. I sort of recognized some of them, but most of them were the quiet, brainy kind of students. You know, the opposite of me.

The little guy with a plaid shirt stood at the front of the class.

"Hello!" he said cheerfully. Then he flashed

me a puzzled smile. "I'm Ronald Rheece, math-club president."

I nodded. "My name's Blue. What's happening?"

"Not much," he answered. "Uh . . . are you sure you belong here?"

"Yeah, yeah," I said, nodding again. "This is the math club, right?"

His smile widened. "It sure is. We're voting on a topic to present at the statewide math fair next month."

"Cool," I said, as if I went to math fairs all the time.

"So, do you want to join us?" Ronald asked. "Is that why you're here?"

"That's why I'm here," I replied.

Ronald motioned toward an empty chair. "Great! We've got some very exciting ideas. Most of us are in the calculus class at the high school. But you can be in our group anyway. Anybody can."

"Thanks." I swallowed. The words *calculus* and *high school* made me a little nervous. But whatever. I'd get the hang of it. I sat down and stretched out my legs to get comfortable. So far, joining clubs wasn't hard at all.

"Ooh, Ronald! Ronald!" A long-haired girl was stamping her feet and waving to get his attention. "I think we should estimate and graph the difference in paper waste if we turned in assignments using both sides of the paper instead of just one side."

One of the other kids shook his head. "One of the high schools did that last year, Francie."

Ronald cleared his throat. "We still have my idea, to calculate the monthly cost of owning a horse versus a car—factoring in the rate of inflation."

Factoring in the what? I couldn't follow any of this. With all the brains in this room, you'd think that they would actually talk about something that made sense.

"Um, you guys mind if I say something?" I asked.

Everybody nodded eagerly. That made me feel good. They might be a little weird, but they were all supernice.

"I don't want to bag on your ideas or anything." I cleared my throat and forced a smile. "But, well, they sound sort of, um, boring."

"Boring?" Ronald repeated. He frowned.

"Okay, well, not boring," I said quickly. "But it's just that, you know, regular people like me aren't going to get into conversions and stuff like that." I brushed my hand over my short hair and looked around at the group. "I mean, this is a *fair,* right? You want to put on a show. You want to do something totally original, something that'll blow people out of the water."

Ronald's expression softened a little. "That is our main objective," he admitted.

I leaned back in the chair. "So we gotta do something fun," I said.

Nobody said a word. All I got in response was a bunch of blank stares.

Maybe I needed to spell it out a little more. These kids seemed a little out of touch. "Okay," I continued. "Like what if you calculate the height of the ramp needed to jump over a Volkswagen Beetle—no, wait, two—on a skateboard? That should involve a lot of intense math, right? And then I could do a demonstration on my skateboard. *That* would be rad."

Most of the kids started smiling. Including Ronald.

"Yeah. What Blue's talking about would involve calculating probable speeds, inertia, angles," he said. "We'd have to allow for all sorts of variables. I say we go for it."

I hopped up and gave Ronald a high five. "Yo, Ron," I said. "Thanks, bro."

He glanced at the rest of the club. "Let's take a vote. All in favor . . ."

Ten hands went up.

"It's unanimous, then," Ronald stated in a

serious voice. "We'll go with Blue's idea."

Everybody clapped. A huge smile broke out on my face. How easy was *that?* Now I was feeling great. This club thing was going to be a breeze.

"Awesome," I said. "You guys are gonna totally rule for sure." My eyes wandered up to the clock. Seven-twenty. I should get going if I wanted to join some *more* clubs. At this rate, I'd probably be president of the school by the end of the day. Then that social worker would never have to come knocking on our door again.

Lacey

"And now we need to discuss feminine hygiene," Miss Scarlett, our gym teacher, announced.

I rolled my eyes and slumped back in the bleachers. Just my luck. Was I cursed or something? As it stands, gym is not my favorite class of the day. Miss Scarlett is a total freak. But did she have to choose *today* to deliver her lecture on menstruation?

Miss Scarlett frowned down at us. "Now, who in this class has had her 'monthly visitor' stop by?"

I raised my arm, trying to look as bored as possible. All the other girls shot their hands into the air too. Of course. No one would be caught dead with her hand down. Miss Scarlett is always happy to single out the "late bloomers" in the group. But I couldn't help glancing at Bethel, who was sitting right next to Jessica Lamefield. Bethel met my gaze for a second, then looked away. She didn't glare, exactly, but she didn't smile either.

Had she told *anybody* about what had happened?

My stomach ached, and it wasn't from cramps. *I hate this,* I thought. *I hate knowing Bethel has the power to practically ruin my whole life.*

". . . and as you all know, girls, hygiene is absolutely vital," Miss Scarlett was droning on.

I pretended to stare down at my feet, but I secretly watched Bethel out of the corner of my eye. She leaned over to Jessica and whispered something in her ear. Jessica put a hand over her mouth like she was trying not to laugh out loud.

Uh-oh. My stomach dropped. I sucked in a breath, but I couldn't let it out again. I got this weird, light-headed feeling, and my hands started to shake. *Bethel just told her. I know it. I'm going to have to move to another school. No . . . another state. Maybe another country.*

I sat there, waiting for Jessica to look at me and start cracking up.

But she didn't. She just stared at Miss Scarlett with a deathly bored expression, like everybody else.

After a few seconds I was able to breathe again. My hands stopped shaking. Bethel had kept her mouth shut. *Again.* And this had been the perfect opportunity to destroy my life. But why was she being so cool?

Not that it mattered, really. What did matter was that my life at SVJH was not over.

Blue

SPANISH CLUB MEETING
HERE DURING 1ST LUNCH!

Finally, I thought. I'd been wandering the school all morning in search of clubs, but I hadn't had any luck since my math-club score. The classroom door was closed, but I could hear a muffled conversation in Spanish. First lunch had already started. I was a little late and a little hungry, but I knew I should really do this. Besides, Spanish club could be cool. I didn't speak Spanish very well, but I could always use it on surfing trips to Mexico with Leaf.

I hurried into the room and closed the door behind me as quietly as I could. This club was definitely more popular than the math club. There must have been twenty kids there. I only had a second to look, but I didn't recognize anybody except this girl on the track team. I see her out running all the time when I'm playing volleyball. I kind of remembered her running for class president too, I think. Her name's really different. Beth? No, Bethel. Bethel McCoy. She'd know what was up with this club. And I was going to need the help, seeing as everybody was talking in Spanish.

I slipped into the empty seat right behind her.

Mr. Enrico, the Spanish teacher, was sitting at his desk, writing something down on a pad. *"Ahora necesitamos decidir lo que vamos a llevar a la fiesta en dos semanas,"* he said quickly.

A dark-haired guy in front of Bethel raised his hand. *"Yo traigo bizcochitos."*

Bethel raised her hand. *"Yo traigo* soda," she said.

I tried to smile. So far, though, Spanish club was bumming me out. All I understood were the words *go, party,* and *soda.* And *soda* didn't exactly count.

I tapped Bethel on the shoulder. "My Spanish kind of stinks," I whispered. "What are they talking about?"

She gave me a funny look, but then she shrugged. "We're having a party in two weeks, so we're all telling what we're going to bring. We've been studying cooking and food for our vocabulary this last unit, so we're supposed to answer in Spanish."

"Thanks," I whispered.

I was in serious trouble here. I thought hard,

trying to remember any Spanish words I could.

Finally it was my turn. I took a deep breath and tried to string together some words that made sense. *"Yo traigo seis personas desnudas,"* I managed to say. It didn't sound half bad either. My accent was pretty decent.

A couple of kids burst out laughing. I swallowed. Mr. Enrico was glaring at me for some reason.

I tapped Bethel on the shoulder again. "What did I say?" I whispered.

Bethel leaned close to me. "You just said you'd bring six naked people," she whispered.

Oh, brother. I sank down in my seat as low as I could.

"How about if I just bring chips?" I suggested.

Bethel

I was closing my locker door when Lacey walked up to me. I tried not to groan. I'd had just about enough of Lacey Frells. When she'd glared at me this morning during Miss Scarlett's lecture, I knew what she was thinking. She was *sure* I would tell Jessica about her getting her first period.

But she doesn't get it. Unlike her, I don't enjoy making other people unhappy. Not even total brats.

"What's up?" I asked. My voice was flat, but I couldn't help it.

She frowned. But then, Lacey is always frowning. I think she thinks it's cool to act like everything in the world is just too boring for her. Her hands were stuffed in the pockets of these really baggy camouflage pants. Then she glanced up and down the hall. It was relatively empty. "So, um, thanks for, you know, not saying anything," she mumbled.

I shrugged, but I was surprised. I'd never

heard Lacey say thank you before in my life. "No problem," I said.

For a few seconds she just stood there, fidgeting. Then she stared down at the floor. "So I was wondering," she whispered. "Do you have any more of those . . . things?"

Of course. I should have known she'd come back to me. I was probably the only person at school who knew her secret. But I guess I felt kind of sorry for her. "Sure," I said. I unzipped my backpack and yanked out the last two pads from the bottom of the bag. "Here you go."

"Thanks." She quickly snatched them away and shoved them into her pocket. Her expression was very uncertain, which is completely un-Lacey-like. "So . . . um, do you always use pads?"

"Yup," I replied. "My mom buys them for me."

Lacey's eyes darted quickly away. "Lucky you," she muttered.

What was *that* supposed to mean? I scowled, but then I remembered: Kristin once told me that Lacey's mom is out of the picture. *And* Lacey hates her stepmom. So she probably had nobody to turn to. I couldn't imagine not having my mom around, especially when it comes to girlie stuff.

"Look, I'm going to the mall after school with

Kristin and Jessica and Brian to get things for the carnival," I found myself saying. "If you want, we could go to the drugstore together then and get you some more pads."

She hesitated, like she really had to think this over. Like if she thought it would be bad for her image to be seen with us in public. I resisted the urge to storm away. Then she let out a big sigh. "Whatever. I guess I could maybe do that."

She made it sound like some horrible chore. Still, I could see the appreciation in her eyes. She *did* need somebody.

Maybe that's why I offered to help. Or maybe I'm just dumb.

Blue

"Hey, Blue, missed you at lunch, dude," Rick yelled across the hall between classes.

I paused and shook my head. "I couldn't go," I muttered.

"Too bad." He snaked his way through the crowd and patted me on the shoulder. "It was hamburgers today. You can still catch the end of second lunch, though."

No, I can't. My shoulders sagged. I *love* hamburgers. I was getting thrashed on all these meetings. But I had to rack up some more memberships. My list for the social worker wasn't even close to long enough yet. Every time I thought about it, my stomach tightened up in a ball.

"So where were you?" he asked.

I shrugged. "A meeting."

Rick squinted at me. "A *school* meeting?"

"Uh-huh."

He took a step closer and looked right into

my eyes. "Dude, are you feeling okay?"

"Not exactly," I admitted, lowering my eyes. I knew he was waiting for me to tell him what was going on, but what was I going to say? *I've totally messed up my life because I'm such a slacker?*

Rick shrugged. "If you want to talk about it, come find me." He patted me again, then took off down the hall. "Later."

"Later," I mumbled. I watched him turn the corner, feeling like an invisible black cloud had just descended over my head. Life was so easy for guys like Rick. And such a bummer for guys like me. I shuffled down the hall, feeling pretty sorry for myself—and angry too because I *never* feel sorry for myself. I had to snap out of this funk.

And then I saw her.

Elizabeth Wakefield. She was sitting in the classroom by the top of the stairs, and on the door was a sign: Carnival Committee—Meet Here During Second Lunch! I smiled. Yes! This was perfect. It was almost like karma or something. She hadn't been in either of the clubs I'd joined so far. In fact, I'd been kind of surprised. I'd thought she'd belong to most of the clubs in school.

I hesitated a second. I had English this period, but I could afford to be a little late. Sure.

As I stepped through the door, I couldn't help but notice that Elizabeth looked kind of different. Her hair was in a long ponytail: a new style for her. And she was wearing more makeup than she usually does. She still looked totally cute, though.

I slipped into the seat behind her and tapped her on the shoulder. "Hey, Liz."

She turned around. "I'm Jessica," she answered dully.

Whoops. My cheeks reddened. I knew Elizabeth had a twin; she'd told me that one time at volleyball. Guess I forgot. "Oh, sorry."

Jessica turned around, flipping her hair back off her shoulder. "It's okay. Happens all the time."

So much for karma. I sank down in my chair. Now I was bummed. I'd been looking forward to seeing Elizabeth all morning. Maybe I should just get out of here and try to grab a burger. But before I could move, a kind of chubby girl with a cute face and really pretty blond curls rushed into the room and slammed the door behind her.

I swallowed. Now I was stuck.

"Hi, guys," she exclaimed breathlessly. "We've got a lot to decide today about the decorations." She grabbed a clipboard and a pen from the

teacher's desk. "First, we have to decide if we
want a balloon arch at the entrance or bunches
of balloons."

"An arch, definitely," Jessica called out.

"Yeah, arch," a girl in front of her agreed.

I tapped Elizabeth's sister lightly on the shoulder and pointed at the girl leading the meeting.
"What's that girl's name again?" I whispered.

Jessica turned around. Her nose wrinkled like
I'd said something totally off the wall. "Kristin?"
she muttered. "Kristin Seltzer? She's only our
class president." Something in the sour tone of
her voice seemed to add the word *duh*.

I sank back into my chair and tried to smile.
"Oh yeah," I said, nodding as if I'd just sort of
forgotten that for a second. "Right." I couldn't
help thinking that Jessica might look exactly like
her sister, but she wasn't the same. At all.

Kristin looked over the crowd. "Anybody
else?" she asked. When nobody said anything,
she made a check on her list. "Okay, balloon
arch," she said.

Wow, she sure did have a lot of energy. And
she seemed so . . . organized. Like Elizabeth, in
a way. How do people do that? I can't even remember my homework most of the time. Not
that I would do it if I did.

"Ms. Upton is going to be our fortune-teller,"

Kristin explained. "What about decorations for her booth?"

Bethel McCoy raised her hand. "I bet the costume shop downtown rents crystal balls," she suggested.

"My mom has these silky tablecloths she'd let us use to drape over the table inside the tent," somebody else said.

Now, this club could be fun. I raised my hand. "Maybe we could get a *real* spiritualist," I offered. "My brother knows this psychic woman who tells people about their past lives. She might be into giving readings at the carnival."

All of a sudden everybody froze, like somebody had pressed a giant pause button. From the front of the room Kristin gave me sort of a blank look. I felt myself blush for about the millionth time that day. Obviously they didn't know about past lives.

"It's really cool," I tried to explain. "Like I found out I was this sailor on one of Columbus's ships. I fell overboard before they got to the Americas, though. Kind of a bummer. She told me that's why I surf. I'm working out my karma about water. It's pretty radical."

Jessica suddenly turned around. She was smirking—and staring at me as if I were insane. Somebody in front of her laughed.

Whatever. If they didn't want to believe it, that was *their* problem. Lots of people are afraid of reincarnation. That's because they're too up-tight to get in touch with other energies.

"That's, um, very interesting, Blue," Kristin finally said. "But we don't really have room in the gym for another booth."

I shrugged. "That's cool," I mumbled. "Maybe next year."

She smiled at me. "Maybe," she said in this kind of small voice. She turned her attention to the rest of the group. "All right, gang. We're going to meet at the mall after school to run a few last-minute errands."

I flipped open my notebook and added that to my to-do list. But on the inside cover I caught a glimpse of the list of all the clubs I'd joined. Only three, counting the carnival one. I got that tight feeling in my stomach again. *Three clubs isn't enough.* Still, what else was there? I tapped the end of my pen against my front teeth, thinking. The day was going to be over soon, and I was missing English—but if I hurried, I might be able to sneak into one more meeting before the next bell rang. Weren't there any more clubs that met at lunch?

Then I got an idea. I added it to my to-do list. *Check out that club that hangs out in the hallway.*

75

Lacey

"This is so boring," Darla Simmons grumbled.

"Totally," I agreed. I leaned back on the bench and looked at the clock at the end of the short corridor—Eyeball Alley, as we call it. We'd been discussing all the dorks who walked by during lunch. That's what Eyeball Alley is for. The cool kids sit on the benches, and the losers walk by us. But even that was getting way old. I can only stand hanging around junior-high kids just so long before I'm ready to scream. Even the cool kids.

I was thinking about ditching fifth and sixth and seeing if Gel, my boyfriend, would drive over and pick me up.

All of a sudden somebody sat next to me. My eyes bulged. Nobody *ever* sits in Eyeball Alley unless they're invited. I couldn't believe who it was. That lame surfer guy. Blue Spiccoli.

"Hey," he drawled in that ridiculous laid-back voice of his. "So what exactly do you guys do?"

he asked me, as if he thought I'd actually answer him. "Do you have an adviser or anything?"

An adviser? What was he talking about? I glared at him and turned away without saying a word. Clearly he was insane. I just hoped he wasn't dangerous or anything.

"Um . . . what do you guys do?" he asked again.

I turned to him. What did he *think* we did? We made fun of dorks like him. It was almost funny, in a way. Did somebody put him up to this on a dare or something? I was thinking about telling him to get lost when Ronald Rheece, supernerd of the universe, tried to sneak by.

Darla sat forward. "Why don't you wear those pants a little higher?" she yelled out.

Spiccoli shook his head. "No way, dude," he said to Ronald. "Don't do it. They're kinda high already, man."

Rheece looked stunned. Then he grinned at Mr. Surf Dork and practically skipped off down the hall.

Now I was starting to get annoyed. *Nobody* comes to Eyeball Alley and ruins our good time. *Nobody.* I turned to face Blue. "What do you think you're doing here?" I demanded.

"Am I doing something wrong?" he asked innocently.

Huh? I was so stunned, I couldn't even say anything at first. But then I nodded.

"Yes," I informed him.

He blinked. "What?" he asked.

"You're *here,*" I said really slowly, so his teeny brain could get it. "And this is where *we* hang out. With our *friends.*" I emphasized the last word, just so he would know that it didn't mean *him.*

"You mean, you're not a school club?" he asked. His eyes were wide. His cheeks were a little pink too.

I threw back my head and laughed. "A *club?*" I cried. "What planet are you from, Spiccoli?"

Darla started cracking up.

Without another word he got up and slunk down the hall.

Finally, I thought, staring at him. What a freak! I couldn't *wait* to be in high school, like Gel. With normal people. Junior high was getting way too weird for me.

Elizabeth

"This is not funny," I grumbled, waving my history book in front of Brian.

But he just laughed. "Yeah, it is."

We were at our locker after school, and I'd just figured out he had switched all of my book covers around. I had to open each book to see what it was. Brian loves practical jokes almost as much as Salvador does, which is just a little too much for me to handle.

"All right, Brian, why don't you just—"

"Hey, you guys!" a voice interrupted me.

I turned to see Blue's friend Rick running down the hall toward us, grinning. "I was looking for you two," he called. "A bunch of us are going to go hang out at the beach for a while. You should come."

Wow, I thought. Hanging out with Blue and his friends the other night had been such a blast, and I was worrying it was only going to be a onetime thing. But now they were looking for us to join them. And it wasn't even Blue. It was one of his friends. I hugged my history book to my chest. "Sure," I said without thinking.

"Me too," Brian added quickly.

"Cool," Rick said. "Let's go."

I turned to close our locker door and caught a glimpse of all my schoolbooks. *But you've got homework,* a silent voice reminded me. My shoulders slumped. I stood there, chewing my lip. "What's wrong?" Brian asked.

"Nothing," I mumbled. "It's just . . . Maybe I shouldn't come. I've got tons of studying."

Brian rolled his eyes and slammed our door shut, as if to hide the books from me. "So what? Do it later."

"But—"

He nudged me with his shoulder. "Come on. What's the worst thing that could happen, you get an A-minus on your history quiz?"

I smirked. He was right. I did take school pretty seriously, but I didn't want Blue's friends to think I was some kind of geek or something. Besides, what if I didn't go and they decided not to ask me again? This could be my one chance.

"Is Blue coming?" I asked.

Rick shrugged. "I guess so. He usually hangs out with us after school, but I hardly saw him today." He tilted his head, as if he was thinking about something. "It's kind of weird, really. He didn't even eat lunch with us. When I saw him in the hall, he was running to some meeting."

"A *meeting?*" I asked. It was kind of hard to believe. From what I knew of Blue, school activities were definitely not a priority. Anyway, he was probably meeting with the surfing club or something. I could just hear him too when I didn't show up at the beach, laughing about how I can get so uptight about my school responsibilities.

But I could prove him wrong. Here was my chance to show him I wasn't always boring and ultraresponsible.

"Okay, I'll come," I agreed. "I just need to call my mom and ask. I'm sure it'll be okay as long as I'm home by dinner."

"Awesome," Rick said.

Brian gave me a wink and a thumbs-up.

I walked in between the two of them as we headed down the hall. It was strange. I couldn't help but feel different around Blue's friends . . . more relaxed, more carefree. I almost wondered if I looked different to other people. All my other friends know me as Miss I'm-involved-in-school.

But maybe I was changing. For the better.

Blue Spiccoli's Thursday To-Do List

1. Join math club. ✔
2. Join Spanish club. ✔
3. Join carnival committee. ✔
4. Join hallway club (mistake—never mind).
5. Read and comment on Lewis Carroll poem "Jabberwocky," due Monday.
6. Find English book! (Look in Rick's locker.)
7. Math test tomorrow on ~~fractions~~ ~~decimals~~
8. Ask Liz what's on math test.
9. Read social-studies chapters and outline ~~important~~ Just read them.
10. Woodworking—make birdhouse, cutting board, and pencil box—due Friday.
11. Oh no.

Kristin

Where on earth is Brian? I wondered for about the hundredth time in five minutes.

I glanced around Toy Joy, the closest thing Sweet Valley Mall has to a party store. All the bright colors and streamers and stuffed animals and balloons weren't doing much to keep me calm. It was way too claustrophobic in here. I was very close to stressing out. Okay, I was already there. Almost the whole committee had come to the mall after school to help buy the decorations, but they were all over the store, goofing off. And Brian hadn't even bothered to show up. He hadn't made it to the meeting at lunch either.

All those paranoid thoughts I had when he was talking about hanging out with Blue Spiccoli came back in a flash. My stomach knotted up. What if Brian *did* think I was boring, the way I get so into school activities—

There he is!

He walked right through the door. . . . No,

wait. It wasn't him. It was . . . *Blue?* What was he doing here?

Blue caught my eye and waved. "Hey," he said. "I've come to help out."

My jaw dropped. I felt like I had entered some kind of bizarro, alternate universe. *Brian* was blowing me off, but his new friend, Blue, was here to help me out. If I tried to figure this one out, I'd just go crazy. I made myself get my mind back on the carnival.

"You guys?" I called to Jessica, Bethel, and the others. "This place doesn't have napkins and tablecloths in our school colors. We need a new plan."

The group members finally managed to straggle over. Blue was with them. I tried not to stare at him.

"What do you have in mind?" Bethel asked.

I studied the clipboard that was becoming my life. "We've got to figure out another color scheme so that the balloon arch will match. What do you guys think about green and white?"

Jessica frowned. "Kind of boring. I don't think white will show up that well in the white gym. What about something more catchy, like blue and purple?"

I glanced at her. "Don't you think that'll make

the whole place look like a big bruise?" I asked. "How about blue and green?"

"Okay." Jessica nodded. "That works."

Blue just grinned.

Bethel shrugged. "Sure," she said. She sounded distracted, and her eyes were on the entrance to the store, as if she was looking for someone. But that was fine. She and I usually argued about every little detail. I just wanted to get our supplies without any problems.

"Okay, so—"

"Hey, guys, check this stuff out," Blue blurted out. He pointed at one of the shelves—straight at a brightly colored pin-the-tail-on-the-donkey game. "This is totally cool," he said. Was he kidding? I almost laughed. *Yeah, it was cool. When we were five.*

"And look at these." He shifted his finger to a bag of black plastic spider rings in front of my nose. "These things rock."

"Blue, we really don't have time for this," I said as nicely as I could. "I only have money to get what we have on the—"

I broke off in midsentence. My totally weird day had just gotten about a thousand times weirder. *Lacey* was here. I blinked, just to make sure I wasn't seeing things. No—there she was, hanging out by the door.

She gave me a tiny nod. "Hey."

"Hi," I said, puzzled. Maybe she actually wanted to help. Maybe she'd finally realized how important the carnival was to me.

Yeah, right. Who was I kidding? Victoria had probably forced her to come here to buy something for Penelope.

And then . . . no, it *couldn't* be. I saw her nod to Bethel. And I could have sworn Bethel nodded back. Bethel, her sworn enemy. Okay. The stress was clearly getting to my head. I had to focus on getting the supplies and getting out of the mall. And then going to bed for about twenty straight hours.

"Let's split up and try to get the stuff we need at other stores, okay?" I asked everyone.

Bethel suddenly slapped her palm against her forehead. "Oh, wait," she said, backing toward the door. "I just remembered something. I'll be right back." She ran out into the hall.

And then I saw the unthinkable.

Lacey followed her. She ran and caught up with her, and the two disappeared around a corner.

I rubbed my eyes. Either I was going crazy, or I was in the midst of a very strange dream. Because there was no possible way Lacey Frells and Bethel McCoy had just ditched me. *Together.*

Lacey

I smirked when Bethel and I pushed open the doors of the drugstore. I couldn't help it.

"What is it?" she asked. She sounded annoyed.

I shrugged. "Nothing." No way I was going to tell Miss Goody-goody that the last time I'd been here, I'd swiped three bottles of nail polish and a pair of silver earrings. She'd probably throw a fit. Not that I had any intention of swiping something *now*. I wanted this experience to be as quick and painless as possible.

Clearly Bethel did too. She headed straight for the aisle with all the feminine-hygiene products. But once we turned the corner, I saw two old ladies and a mom with a little kid there.

No way, I thought. This was embarrassing enough without an audience. I grabbed Bethel's arm and made her stop. "Let's check out the makeup until they're gone," I whispered.

"Whatever," she said, rolling her eyes. But she followed me over to the lipstick section. For a minute she stood there, tapping her foot impatiently while I tried a couple of different colors on the back of my hand.

Finally the aisle emptied.

Bethel led the way without a moment's hesitation. She stopped right in front of all the pads. "Okay," she said, "I guess I should explain all this stuff before somebody else shows up."

I glanced up and down the aisle. "Yeah, fine. Whatever," I mumbled nervously.

She picked up a pink box. "These are minipads," she explained. "They're smaller and thinner than regular pads. Some of them have wings, which means they sort of hang down the sides. Don't use these except for when your period's almost over. They're too small otherwise."

"Okay, okay." I stared at the rows of boxes. I *hated* having all this explained to me. It made me feel like a stupid baby. Plus I just knew Bethel was going to start making fun of me any second for not knowing any of this.

She put the minipad box back and tapped a larger box with her finger. "These are the kind of pads I gave you. That's what I'd get if I were you. It says there are thirty in here. I usually use a few a day, so that should last you for a long time."

"Thanks," I muttered. I couldn't believe she hadn't started ragging on me yet.

I watched her checking out the boxes. She wasn't sneering, or pretending not to laugh . . . or *anything*. Maybe she actually wasn't planning on making fun of me.

A box of tampons caught my eye. I pointed at them. "So why don't you use these?"

"My mom won't let me," Bethel replied. "She says I have to wait until I'm older."

Older sounded good. Older meant more mature. Maybe I'd go for those. "Why does she say that?" I asked.

"Because you have to be more careful," Bethel replied. "If you don't change them properly, you could get an infection."

I studied the box. *Ick*. I didn't want an infection. As much as I hated to admit it, I was kind of impressed with how Bethel said things in such a straightforward way. Most girls would be so totally embarrassed, they couldn't talk. "Okay . . . so . . . I guess I'll get the pads, then," I stated.

I looked at the boxes of full-sized pads. There were a bunch of different brands. "Why do these have such lame names?" I wondered out loud.

Bethel grinned. "I know. Who thought of

Spring Breeze for something you stick in your underwear?"

"Really." I rolled my eyes. "So what do I want?" I asked, pretending to be all serious. "Spring Breeze, Freedom, or All Day Fresh?"

We both giggled.

Amazingly enough, this wasn't nearly as bad as I'd expected. I grabbed a box of pads off the shelf and headed toward the front of the store. There were three checkout people, but only one was a woman. She had the longest line too. But there was no way I would stick these up on the counter in front of some high-school guy or an old man.

I looked at Bethel.

"Stand back there," she said, pointing at another aisle. "I'll tell you when the lady's free."

Wow. Now I was *really* impressed. Bethel knew exactly what I was thinking, and I didn't even have to tell her. I hid around the corner behind the toilet-paper display to wait. I couldn't believe how embarrassing this was: hiding out in a drugstore with a dork like Bethel McCoy. But at least I would be able to do it on my own next time.

A minute later Bethel's head appeared around the aisle.

"It's safe," she whispered, motioning with her hand.

I hurried over to the lady's cash register and paid for the pads as quickly as I could—almost forgetting to get my change. Then I made sure the top of the paper bag was folded over so no one could see inside and walked out the door.

Bethel followed me. She hesitated, then turned to head back toward Toy Joy.

I cleared my throat. "Okay," I said.

She stopped and frowned at me.

"So, you know, thanks for, you know . . . whatever," I muttered, staring down at the floor.

"You're welcome," she said matter-of-factly.

I watched as she walked away. I couldn't help feeling mildly shocked. Bethel had helped me. *Me.* Without laughing in my face or making me feel like a baby. I started heading for the exit. The question was: Why? Bethel's helping me made no sense at all. My good luck, I guess. It was best not to worry about it. It was best not to *think* about it. Nope. I'd just ditch the box of pads under the sink in my bathroom, then maybe head over to Gel's and bum a cigarette. I definitely needed one.

Messages on the Wakefields' Answering Machine

Hi, this is Anna calling for Liz. Liz, it's almost four. Where were you after school today? I wanted to talk to you about an idea I had for *Zone*. Call me, okay?

Beep.

Hi, Elizabeth, it's Salvador. Are you ever going to check your e-mail? Are you ever going to come home? Call me tonight. I'll be home after seven.

Beep.

Brian

I was totally exhausted by the time Elizabeth's brother, Steven, dropped me off at home. I never imagined surfing could be so hard. Not that I'd actually surfed. Not technically. I'd basically flailed about in the water while Rick, Jaimie, and Elizabeth laughed at me. But I didn't mind. Even making a fool out of myself with those guys was more fun than I'd had in a long time.

"Hello!" I called as I opened the front door.

"We're in here," Mom answered from the kitchen. "We're about to start dinner."

I hurried up the stairs to my room. "Be right down," I shouted back. I swung my book bag off my shoulder as I threw open the door to my room—then paused. While we were hanging out at the beach, I'd come up with a brilliant idea for my video game: I was going to give the three-headed reptile a spiked tail to use as a weapon. I just wanted to scribble it down before I forgot.

As fast as I could, I unzipped my bag and yanked out my notebook. When I opened it, a piece of white paper fluttered to the ground. I frowned. What was this?

Brian—
Could history be more boring today? I am so hungry, I could scream. Too bad lunch isn't for another hour. Anyway, don't forget we're meeting at the mall after school.
XOXOXO
Kristin

I froze. *The meeting.* I'd completely spaced it. My heart started pounding in my chest. I couldn't believe this. How could I be so stupid? Kristin would never forgive me for bailing on the decorating committee. I crumpled the paper into a ball and dashed to the phone to call her, nearly tripping over all the dirty laundry strewn across the floor.

"Bri-an," my mother called from downstairs.

"Coming!" I cried as I furiously punched in Kristin's number.

She picked up the phone on the first ring. "Hello?"

"Uh . . . hi," I said. My voice was shaking a little.

There was a pause. "Oh," she said. Her voice was colorless. "It's you."

"Look, I am so sorry about the meeting today," I blurted out. "I completely forgot, and I know there's no—"

"That's okay," she interrupted.

I shook my head. "No, it's not."

"Brian!" Billy shouted up the stairs. "Get down here!"

I rolled my eyes and covered the mouthpiece with my hand. "In a second!" I yelled. *Man,* I thought. What was the big deal about starting dinner exactly on time anyway?

Kristin sighed. "Brian, I better go."

"I'm sorry, Kristin," I insisted. "I really want to make it up to you. And you were right. I should have written the mall trip down in my notebook."

"And the lunch meeting," she added.

Oops. I squeezed my eyes shut, feeling queasy. "Right. The lunch meeting. I am *such* a dork. I promise I'll do better and help out."

There was no answer. I held my breath.

"Okay," she said finally.

I let out a big gust of air. *Whew.* I am definitely lucky to have such an understanding girlfriend. "So, did you get all the stuff you needed?"

"Yeah," she said. But she sounded strange—as if she was unsure about something. "The meeting at Toy Joy was pretty weird, though."

My eyes narrowed. "What happened?"

"A lot of stuff," she grumbled. "For one thing, Bethel was acting really strange in the store. Then Lacey showed up for some reason. The next thing I know, the two of them disappear. They *hate* each other. And your friend Blue was there too."

"Blue?" I blinked. That *was* weird. "What was he doing there?"

"He came to the lunch meeting and said he wanted to help," she said.

"Seriously?" I asked.

"I guess." I could hear her breathing on the other end. "Brian?"

"Yeah?"

"If . . . if I was getting, you know, boring or something, you'd tell me, right?

I laughed. "Are you *crazy?* Kristin, you are totally not boring. You're only planning, like, the biggest school function ever. You have a right—"

A loud, fumbling noise cut her off.

"Brian!" Billy's voice barked.

I winced and held the phone away from my ear. Great. My meathead brother was ruining the moment.

"Get down here!" he commanded. "Now!"

"I guess I better go, Kristin," I mumbled. "I'll call you later."

She giggled. "Okay, Brian. Bye."

I hung up the phone. My jaw was tightly clenched. I was angry at Billy. But mostly I was angry at myself. I *had* been irresponsible lately. And this carnival was superimportant to Kristin. *No more missed meetings,* I told myself as I hurried from my room. Surf lessons and three-headed reptiles would just have to wait.

Elizabeth

The instant Anna opened her notebook and pulled out her algebra assignment, I realized what had been nagging at me all morning.

Math homework.

Of course. With all the fun at the beach with Rick and Jaimie and Brian, I'd completely forgotten about it. A peculiar, sickly feeling gnawed at my insides. I leaned back in my seat and glanced at Salvador, who sat on the other side of me. "You guys," I whispered. "I forgot to do my math last night."

Salvador laughed. "Yeah, right." He didn't even bother looking up from his desk.

"I'm serious!" I hissed. I turned back to Anna.

She just frowned at me. "*You* forgot homework? Give me a break."

I shook my head, my eyes widening. "I'm not kidding!"

A few heads turned in my direction. My cheeks burned. Since when had I become such a flake? Salvador leaned across the aisle and grabbed the edge of my desk. He stared deeply into my eyes.

"Send back Elizabeth Wakefield right now," he commanded. "We've seen through your alien disguise."

"This isn't funny," I whispered. I glanced up at the clock. My breath started coming fast. I had about two minutes until class started. "Will you guys help me?"

Salvador wriggled his eyebrows at Anna. "I don't know," he said in a skeptical tone. "She's *so* irresponsible. Should we?"

"Well . . ." Anna pursed her lips. "Maybe just this once," she said, pretending to be serious. She handed me her homework. "You better take mine. Who knows how many Salvador will get right."

"Hey!" Salvador protested. "Math's my best subject."

I ignored them and started scribbling down answers. I couldn't believe I'd sunk this low: copying a friend's homework. Of course, I'd do the same for Anna if *she* was in a jam. But I just felt so *dishonest*—like I was covered in a layer of slime or something. I tried not to think about it.

"Tell me if Ms. Upton comes in," I murmured without looking up.

Salvador snickered. I resisted the urge to reach across the aisle and smack him.

"So, where were you after school yesterday?" Anna asked.

"At the beach," I answered distractedly. The numbers on Anna's page danced before my eyes. I had only three more problems to go.

"The beach?" Salvador repeated. He sounded shocked.

I paused for a second and glanced up at them. "What?"

Anna was frowning at me, her chin propped in her hand. "Since when do you hang out at the beach?"

"I don't know," I muttered, then went back to copying. "I guess since I met some kids on my volleyball team." I rushed through the last problem and handed Anna back her paper, then leaned back in my chair and let out a huge sigh of relief. "Whew. Thanks a lot. I really appreciate it."

But she just kept staring at me. "Did you have a practice or something?"

"No." I shook my head. Gradually my heart slowed to something resembling a normal beat. "I guess they hang out there after school, and they asked me and Brian to go with them."

Anna blinked. "Oh," she said. She shot Salvador a puzzled glance, then turned and faced the front of the classroom.

And I had the best time, I added to myself. I didn't want to say it out loud. Somehow I thought it might hurt their feelings if I told them. They seemed pretty confused by the whole incident as it was. After all, it's always been the three of us: Salvador and Anna and me, ever since I started SVJH. Then again, Anna was making new friends in the drama club. In fact, Anna's drama-club experience had inspired me to try new things.

"Hey, Liz," Salvador said. "We were thinking we should have a *Zone* meeting this weekend."

"Sure," I agreed. "How about Saturday at Vito's?"

Anna nodded. "I can make it."

"Me too," Salvador added. "You want to call Brian?" he asked me.

The tardy bell rang, and Ms. Upton rushed into the room.

"No problem," I whispered.

I glanced over my messy homework copy. I had no idea what the chapter was even about. The weirdest thing was, I should have been worried about missing the assignment, but I wasn't. I was in a great mood, in fact. Hanging out with Blue's friends had been so much fun. Besides, what was one sloppy math paper here or there?

Blue

I was hurrying through the hall toward English class when all of a sudden I freaked out. I *did* have my assignment with me, didn't I? I stopped so fast that the kid behind me slammed right into my back. He groaned. I smiled sheepishly over my shoulder. "Sorry, bro."

"Whatever," the guy muttered. Luckily he was about six inches shorter than I am. He scurried away.

Even though the hall was totally crowded, I slid my backpack off and ripped it open. I *had* to have that assignment. I'd worked really hard on it last night, and I was positive I'd put it in here. I grabbed out handfuls of loose notebook paper and started thumbing through them. I was starting to panic now. I dug into the bottom of my bag for the most crumpled pages.

Yes! There it was, stuck to the back of my history essay with an unwrapped peppermint candy. Wherever *that* had come from. I shook my head, then carefully peeled the pages apart and smoothed them out over my thigh.

"Whew," I muttered out loud.

A couple of girls giggled as they stepped around me, but I didn't even care. I was sort of proud of my work on this assignment. Actually, after that weird trip to the mall yesterday, I'd worked really hard on a *bunch* of homework. Some of it was even kind of cool. Like that "Jabberwocky" poem. The guy wrote gibberish words that sounded like they really meant something. I was even looking forward to seeing what the other kids in class thought about it. I hoped I got it right.

By the time I gathered up all my stuff and scrambled into the classroom, everybody else was already there. I slipped into my seat beside Rick.

"Hey, dude," I whispered. "Didn't you dig that poem?"

He stared at me as if I were crazy. His eyebrows practically rose the whole way up his forehead. "You *read* it?"

I shrugged.

"Wow." He laughed. "I didn't know you even *had* an English book. What's with you and school lately?"

I swallowed and frowned down at my homework paper. For some reason, Rick's question really bummed me out. What was I going to say? *I've blown off school so long, my grades completely suck, and I might get put in a foster home?*

"Is Leaf cracking down on you?" he asked.

"Uh . . . I guess you could say that." I couldn't bring myself to look Rick in the eye. All the excitement over my homework had faded. "Anyway, I just decided, you know, to . . . um, be more responsible."

Rick's jaw dropped. Then he smiled. "Get out of here."

I glared at him. I was starting to get kind of irritated. "You know, we're going to be in high school pretty soon, and grades can be kind of important," I said.

He didn't answer. He just stared at me. "Blue?" he finally asked. "Did you get whacked on the head by a surfboard last night?"

Sure, I thought. *Just keep on joking.* I shook my head. It was easy for him to kid around. He wasn't about to have some stranger snoop through his whole house and judge him.

Bethel

As soon as Mr. Wilfred, the algebra teacher, turned his back to write out a problem on the board, Jessica leaned close to me.

"Why did you and Lacey disappear from the party store together yesterday?" she whispered. "I thought you couldn't stand her."

I'd been expecting this. In fact, I was kind of surprised that nobody had asked me about it earlier. I knew Jessica and Kristin and the rest of the kids had probably seen us leave, so I had my story ready. "Kristin asked us to go get some stuff they didn't have at the party store," I lied.

Jessica wrinkled her nose. "Kristin actually asked you and Lacey to do something together?"

"I know." I made myself laugh. I wished Mr. Wilfred would turn around so we'd have to stop talking. To be honest, I hated lying. And I had a feeling I wasn't that great at it.

Jessica was drawing daisies down the margin of her paper with a pink pen. The ink matched her nail polish. It was sort of funny. How could anyone love the color pink so much? She shook her head. "Kristin's either beyond stressed, or she wanted to get Lacey back for something. She's gotta know that you guys don't get along."

"Kristin's not like that," I said.

"Yeah. I guess you're right." Jessica drew a happy face in the center of one of the daisies. "So what did you and Lacey have to buy?"

I cleared my throat. Luckily I had thought of this. "We need videotapes for the karaoke booth, so we went—" I stopped.

Lacey, late as usual, had sauntered in the back door of the classroom.

And she was staring right at us.

She was close enough that I knew she'd over-heard our conversation. ". . . so we went over to the drugstore," I finished, my eyes on Lacey's face.

Her expression was perfectly blank. No smile, no frown, no glare. She was simply watching Jessica and me.

I gave her a kind of half smile. She almost smiled back. I *think*. Then she put her books down on her desk in the last row.

"Miss Frells, you're late," Mr. Wilfred an-nounced from the front of the room. "See me after class."

Lacey shrugged and sank down in her seat

until her head was resting on the back of her chair. "Whatever."

She sounded completely bored, which, I'm sure, she was. But at that moment she gave me a long look from under half-closed eyelids. Then she lifted her chin just the slightest bit.

I think that was supposed to be a thank-you. I hoped so. I had no intention of telling anybody about what was going on with her, but I really hadn't planned on having to lie either. She *owed* me a thank-you. Big time.

Blue

By the time the ref blew her whistle
to end the game, I thought I was going to col-
lapse. I'd never played harder. I ran myself
ragged—totally acing every serve, totally nailing
every spike. I had to be able to put "star athlete"
down on my list for the social worker. If this
lady was going to invade my life, I wanted
everything to look perfect. *Better* than perfect.

Elizabeth and Rick came running up to me as
the Redwood Middle School team slowly filed
out of the gym. I stared at the Redwood guys.
They looked bummed. Then again, we'd beaten
them pretty badly. I felt kind of strange watching
them, almost like I'd done something wrong.
Normally I'm more into having fun than winning.

"You were awesome!" Elizabeth cried.

"Thanks," I mumbled.

Rick clapped me on the back. "You *ruled*,
dude!"

"Thanks," I said as nicely as I could. "I better go

help Leaf take the net down and stuff." It was cool to be showered with all these compliments—*especially* from Elizabeth—but the faster I helped Leaf clean up the gym, the faster I'd get home so I could start on my homework. Leaf was already unhooking the net from the posts. I hurried over to him.

Elizabeth kind of stood there, watching me. "So, um, I guess I'll see you later," she called.

My shoulders slumped. I'd been playing so intensely that I'd barely even said hi to her. But I couldn't let that get me down. As soon as this social-services stuff was behind me, I could talk to her all I wanted.

"Yeah, see you later," I called back, without turning around. I could hear her tennis shoes squeaking across the wood floor as she walked away. I shook my head. Why was life so unfair sometimes? If I'd only worked harder—

"Pizza at Blue's!" Rick suddenly cried. "Come on, Liz!"

What? My eyes widened. I spun around, but before I could even say anything, he'd grabbed Elizabeth's arm and the two of them were racing for the door.

"You guys!" I shouted. "Wait!"

The door slammed shut behind them. My jaw tightened. What was Rick *doing?* He couldn't just invite himself over like that.

"What's the matter?" Leaf asked.

I shook my head. "Rick just invited himself and Liz over to our house. *That's* what's the matter."

But Leaf just laughed as he finished rolling up the volleyball net. "Rick invites himself over practically every single day," he said.

"But this is different!" I yelled.

Leaf blinked at me. "Why?"

"Because that stupid social worker is coming tomorrow," I growled. "We have to clean the house."

"Aw, come on," Leaf said, grinning. "Cleaning up the house will take two seconds. Anyway, it's a Friday night. Time to chill."

I gaped at him. I couldn't believe the way he was acting. Majorly uncool. *Majorly.* I took a deep breath, struggling to keep control of myself. "What if cleaning the house takes more than two seconds?" I asked through gritted teeth.

Leaf sighed, then put the half-rolled net down on the floor. He came over and put his hand on my shoulder. "Blue, it's gonna be fine, all right? You've totally gotten your act together this past week. That's all that matters. We've never had a problem with the social workers before, remember? This'll be a piece of cake. Trust me."

I wanted to trust him. Like when I was little, and he'd always fix everything. But I couldn't. Not this time. I guess it's a lot easier to believe adults are superheroes when you're five. Then you grow up and learn that you have to get yourself out of your own messes. Which is a complete bummer.

Instant Messages Between Lacey Frells and Kristin Seltzer

KGrl99: Didn't expect to see *you* at Toy Joy.

L88er: Had some time to kill. Gel was picking me up.

KGrl99: So since when are you and Bethel buds?

L88er: Bethel? Yeah, right. Since never.

KGrl99: You ditched me with her. I saw it.

L88er: I didn't ditch you *with* her. I needed a cigarette. I don't know why she left, but I saw her go into the drugstore.

KGrl99: You weren't together?

L88er: Of course not. Look, we're not buds, all right? But she's not as completely irritating and lame as I thought she was.

KGrl99: Are you talking about *Bethel?*

KGrl99: Lacey, are you there still?

L88er: Gotta go.

Elizabeth

"All right, Liz," Jaimie said, dangling her skateboard in front of me. She brushed her long, blond dreads out of her eyes and grinned. "Are you ready to give this thing a try?"

I sat there for a moment on the Spiccolis' big, overstuffed couch, stroking my chin. I *did* want to try skateboarding, but I didn't want to fall down and break my arm or anything. "Maybe after the pizza comes," I said.

"Chicken," Rick teased. He started duck walking around the living room, flapping his arms in a ridiculous chicken dance. *"Bawk!"* he squawked. *"Bawk!"*

Leaf threw a bag of potato chips at his head.

"Hey!" Rick protested, laughing. The bag fell to the carpet.

I gave Leaf a quick thumbs-up. "Thanks."

"Do you *mind?*" Blue demanded. He jumped out of one of the easy chairs and snatched up the bag. "Somebody could step on that."

Rick's laughter faded. He glanced back at Leaf,

then at Blue. "Sorry," he mumbled sheepishly.

"Hey, Blue," Leaf called with an easygoing smile. "It's cool, bro."

Blue didn't say anything. He simply fell back into his chair, clutching the bag of chips and scowling.

I stared at him. What was going on? Why was he in such a bad mood? Last time I was at his house, it was littered with garbage and pizza boxes and soda cans. This time Blue was freaking about a bag of potato chips—that was *closed*.

Now that I thought about it, he had been acting really strange all week. Like at volleyball today. He'd played like he was trying to make the Olympics or something. And all of a sudden he was totally focused on schoolwork and didn't have any time for his friends. Rick said he'd joined just about every club in the school too.

"So who wants something to drink?" Leaf asked loudly, as if he was trying hard to fill the uncomfortable silence that now filled the room.

I raised my hand. Leaf disappeared into the kitchen, then came back a second later and tossed me an orange soda. I grabbed it out of the air and popped it open. I wished I hadn't. Orange fizz exploded from the top of the can, dripping all over my shorts and the beige carpet.

"Whoops!" Jaimie and Leaf yelled at the same time.

"Oh, jeez, I'm so sorry," I said, setting my can down on the coffee table. "Do you have any paper towels?"

"I can't *believe* this!" Blue barked. He stormed past me and headed for the kitchen. "That stuff stains really badly."

I swallowed, not knowing what to do.

"Yo, Blue, man—it was an accident," Jaimie said. "She didn't mean it or anything."

"Whatever," Blue muttered. He rushed back into the living room with a roll of paper towels and carpet cleaner and threw himself down at the stains by my feet.

I bent down beside him. "Here, let me—"

"Just go away, all right?" he interrupted, spraying the orange spots and scrubbing them furiously. "You've done enough damage."

All right. This was too much. I wasn't uncomfortable any longer; I was just plain angry. "What is your problem?" I demanded.

He shot me a cold stare. His blue eyes were like ice. "You shouldn't be drinking in the living room. That's irresponsible." His gaze fell back to the carpet, and he shook his head. "This stuff will never come out."

My cheeks got hot. "Excuse me? *I'm* being

irresponsible? *You're* the one who told me I could do whatever I wanted here, remember?" I stood up and glanced at Leaf. "I'm sorry about the soda, okay?"

Leaf nodded sympathetically. "I know, Liz. It's cool."

"It's *not* cool," Blue snapped. "It's totally not cool." He sighed and glanced around the room. "What are you guys even doing here? Shouldn't we all be doing our homework?"

I burst out laughing. I couldn't help myself. That was the most ridiculous thing I'd ever heard coming from Blue. Until last week it was a miracle if he even made it to school half the time.

Blue wasn't laughing, though. "What's so funny?" he growled.

"*You* are!" I cried. "I mean, you're being so up-tight."

He sneered. "Look who's talking," he snapped.

My laughter instantly stopped. I could feel my anger returning. "Blue, no offense, but I'm not the one telling everyone to go do their homework on a Friday night."

"Right," he said bitterly. "You're all mellow now. Why are you pretending to be totally casual about everything? If you ask me, that's pretty fake."

My jaw practically fell to the floor. "Fake?" I shouted. The veins in my neck bulged, but I couldn't help it. "*You're* the one pretending to be Mr. Honor Roll. *You're* the one—"

"Look, why don't you just get lost?" he spat.

"Fine." Without another word, I stormed out the door. I could feel everyone's eyes on me, but luckily nobody said anything. Hot tears were building up behind my eyeballs. I blinked really hard, fighting them back. One thing was for certain: I'd been very wrong about hanging out with Blue and his friends. It *wasn't* cool. Nope. It wasn't cool at all.

Blue Spiccoli's Saturday Morning

7:30 A.M. Alarm goes off.

7:31 A.M. Hits the snooze button.

8:46 A.M. Wakes up, sees the time, and realizes he turned the alarm off instead of hitting snooze. Flies out of bed.

8:47 A.M. Freezes in panic, thinking about the social worker's surprise visit.

8:48 A.M. Panic attack over.

9:53 A.M. Finishes reading three history chapters. It turns out Benjamin Franklin was kind of a cool guy. An inventor, sort of like Leaf.

9:58 A.M. Scarfs down three cherry Pop-Tarts and checks out the waves from the kitchen window. Luckily the tide is coming in and the surf isn't any good.

9:59 A.M. Looks out over the ocean, remembering the two seconds he spent under the starlight with Elizabeth that first time she came to his house. Immediately stresses about their argument yesterday.

10:01 A.M. Opens his English book and reads the assigned poem, "The Road Less Taken." It's actually way cool. Decides to study more often.

Blue

Being stuck in the mall on Saturday afternoon was *not* good for my stress level. The stupid social worker could show up at the house any minute, and I still had to get a whole bunch of stuff for the carnival committee. I'd already taken care of the math fair, which wasn't easy. It had taken me forever to find a store that sold compasses. I'd finally found them at a place called Nettie's Crafts. I never thought they'd sell compasses at a craft store, but the lady told me they used them for drawing things on fabric and stuff. Whatever. Unfortunately, they didn't have protractors. I didn't have time to get them either. I didn't even really *care* at this point. Ronald and the other kids would just have to go with the flow.

I scratched my head and headed toward Toy Joy. Suddenly I spotted a pay phone. *Hmmm,* I thought. Should I call Leaf again and see if the social worker was there yet? Probably. I ran up and dropped change in the slot, then punched in our number.

Leaf picked up. "Hello?"

"It's me."

He started laughing. "You called ten minutes ago, bro. Mellow out, okay?"

"Fine," I said. I dropped the phone back on the hook. *Mellow out. Yeah, right.* Leaf's attitude was really starting to get on my nerves. *It's only my life. No big deal.*

I took two steps away from the phone—then stopped dead in my tracks.

Elizabeth was walking right toward me.

Oh no. I couldn't move. I couldn't even *breathe.* All the blood in my body seemed to rush to my feet. After the way I'd flipped out on her yesterday, I wondered if she was going to start yelling at me. Well, either that or ignore me. I didn't know which would be worse.

Her eyes met mine. She froze too. She couldn't have been more than ten feet away. For some reason, she was holding a plastic bag with these big feathers sticking out of it.

"Oh," she muttered. "Hey."

"Hey." I tried to smile, but I don't think it worked.

She looked down at her feet, then kept walking.

"Wait, Liz!" I blurted out.

Her lips twisted in a frown. She stopped, but she didn't bother to look up. "Yeah?"

I opened my mouth, but no words would come. How could I apologize for being so rude without completely embarrassing myself? *Sorry I flipped out on you last night, but I've been a complete slacker at school and my grades are, like, Fs, and so this social worker is going to come and check me out to make sure I'm not some kind of idiot who needs to be in a foster home. . . .*

"What's in the bag?" I found myself asking lamely, just to keep talking.

She shrugged. "I'm doing a favor for Jessica. She was supposed to pick up peacock feathers for the fortune-teller's booth, but she's superbusy, so I said I'd do it for her."

"Oh," I said.

Elizabeth sighed and shook her head. "Well, um, I better go. I'm kind of in a hurry." Her voice was very flat. "I'm meeting Salvador and Anna and Brian at Vito's for a *Zone* meeting before the carnival today. I barely have time to take this stuff over to school first."

"I could take those to school for you," I offered automatically, without even thinking.

She finally glanced up at me. Her brow was tightly furrowed. "Really?"

I nodded. "Yeah." I bit my lip. "It's the least I could do for being such a jerk to you yesterday."

Finally her face seemed to soften a little. "Blue—"

"No, really, Liz," I interrupted. "I was way, way out of line. And you're right. I've been totally uptight lately. It's just . . . some things are stressing me out."

She swallowed, looking me in the eye. "It's nothing serious, is it?"

"It could be," I admitted. But in spite of everything, I managed a grin. Elizabeth wasn't yelling at me. She was being really cool, in fact. That was more than I could have hoped for. "I mean it about taking that stuff to school for you, though. I insist."

A full-fledged smile finally spread across her face, sending a warm shiver down my spine. "Thanks, Blue," she murmured. "That would be great."

I couldn't believe how relieved I felt when she handed me the bag. It was like my stress level suddenly got cut in half. For once in the past week I'd actually done something *right*. Coming to the mall was definitely good karma.

"Bye, Blue," she called. She waved and started to walk toward the exit.

I waved back. "Bye." I turned to head for Toy Joy. But then I stopped. The pay phone caught my eye again.

Once more. I'd call Leaf just once more before I left.

I rushed up to the phone, stuffed in more change, and dialed.

"Hello?" Leaf answered.

"Hey."

"She's here, Blue," he whispered.

My stomach plunged. *This is it,* I thought. *The moment of truth.* My heart started rattling so hard that it actually hurt. "Okay," I finally managed to croak. "I'll be home in ten minutes."

I hung up, then stared down at the fringy-looking feathers in the bag Elizabeth had given me. *Oh no.* My shoulders sagged. There was no way I had time to stop at school now. But what could I do? I could either blow off Elizabeth's favor or possibly lose my home. It was kind of a no-brainer.

I just hoped Elizabeth wouldn't hate me forever.

Kristin

My insides were in knots. I paced my room. It was almost one o'clock. Why hadn't anyone called yet? They should have called hours ago. All of us should have been at the gym decorating already. There wasn't going to be enough time to get everything set up before the carnival started. I just *knew* it. We had to get going too. Maybe I needed to make the first move. After all, I was in charge. Maybe they thought that I was supposed to call *them,* so they were all at home, waiting for me. . . .

I grabbed the phone off my nightstand and dialed Brian's number.

The phone seemed to ring forever. I tapped my foot on the floor impatiently.

"Hello?" he finally answered.

"Hi, it's me," I said. "When can you meet me at school? We've got a million things to set up. We should go as soon as we can."

There was a long pause. "I sort of have a problem," he mumbled. "I totally forgot about

124

this huge English paper I have to write for Monday. I meant to do it this week, but since we've been hanging out at Blue's house and everything, I never got started."

Ha, ha, ha, I thought, frowning. Sometimes Brian's sense of humor lacks comic timing. "Look, just—"

"Oh no," he interrupted.

"What?"

"That's not all." His voice was shaky. "I totally forgot. I have a *Zone* meeting in an hour."

My grip tightened around the phone. "You're not joking, are you?"

"I wish," he grumbled.

I felt like screaming. "You *promised* me you'd help!"

"I know, I know." He sighed loudly. "Listen, I'll get Billy to drive me over to school right after the meeting, okay?"

Unbelievable. I shook my head. He sounded like helping with this carnival was the last thing on earth he wanted to do.

"Kristin?" he asked.

"Yes?" I snapped.

"Don't stress out so bad about this, okay? It'll work out."

My eyes smoldered. "I am not stressing. You promised. I mean, I just . . ." I took a deep breath. I was so flustered that I couldn't even speak. "You know, if you hadn't been spending so much time with Blue Spiccoli and the rest of the volleyball gang—"

"So I have other friends," he cut in. He sounded angry. "I hate to tell you, but not everybody is so totally into this carnival, you know."

"Then don't even bother to come," I replied shortly. "I'm hanging up now."

"Me too."

"Fine," I yelled, and slammed down the phone.

For all I cared, Brian could spend the rest of his life with those slackers. I had a carnival to organize—with or without a pathetic boyfriend to help me. And it was going to be the best carnival anyone had ever been to.

Blue

Just open the door, I commanded myself.

Easier said than done. My knees were shaking so badly, I could hardly move. But finally I reached up and turned the knob. The door swung open. I stepped inside, then paused.

Wait a second.

Somebody was *laughing*. A woman. Could it be the social worker? I dropped the bags from the mall right there by the door and stepped into the living room.

Then I nearly collapsed.

This was *not* our home.

For one thing, it smelled like a new car instead of like pizza and old surfboard wax. Leaf's sailfish had disappeared too. A gigantic painting of a lighthouse hung in its place. Even our ratty, comfy old couch had been covered with a new blue spread or something. Leaf and an older woman in an official-looking suit strolled out of the kitchen. Her dark hair was in a tight bun. Both of them were smiling.

My eyes bulged. Leaf had cut his hair! I couldn't believe it. No more sun-bleached, shoulder-length curls. And he was dressed in *slacks*. A long-sleeved, button-down shirt hid his tattoos. He'd even taken off the old friendship bracelets he'd been wearing for years. He looked like a lawyer or something.

Whoa. All I could do was stare.

Leaf grinned and gave me a quick wink. "Hi, Blue," he said. "This is Ms. Willard."

The lady walked right up to me and extended a hand. I shook it vigorously.

"Hello, Blue," she said. "Your brother has been telling me a lot about you."

"Uh-oh," I mumbled.

She laughed. "Don't worry."

Yeah, right, I thought, but I made myself smile. *You try not worrying at a time like this.*

"Why don't we go sit in the living room?" Leaf suggested.

"Good idea," the woman replied. She eased herself down on the newly covered couch. Leaf and I both sat in easy chairs. I couldn't help but notice that Leaf had tossed a little throw rug over Elizabeth's orange-soda stains. It was amazing. He'd thought of everything.

For what seemed like a long time, we just sat there, smiling at each other. My leg kept bouncing up and down. I couldn't stop it. I was way too nervous.

"So, why don't you tell me about school, Blue?" Ms. Willard suggested.

"Sure." I perched on the edge of the chair and folded my hands in my lap. "School's great. Oh, in fact, I've got to leave soon. I'm on the decorating committee for the big carnival today, and we have to set things up."

She nodded approvingly. "That's wonderful. And what classes are your favorites?"

I thought for a second. "English is pretty cool. We just read this poem 'Jabberwocky.' Really outstanding."

"Oh yes!" She smiled at me. Now that I noticed, she had a really nice face—very kind and motherly. I relaxed a little. "I remember reading that poem too," she said. "Your brother tells me you're pretty active in clubs as well."

"Definitely." I glanced over at Leaf. I had to hand it to him, he'd really done a great job. He was cool as cool could be. "I, uh, belong to a bunch of clubs, actually. Let me get my list. It's in my backpack." I jumped up and headed for the hall closet, where I'd put it last night when I was cleaning up.

"Blue, no!" Leaf suddenly yelled.

Too late. I yanked open the closet door. The

next thing I knew, a ton of junk was falling on my head—including Leaf's sailfish. *Oh no. Oh no . . .* So *this* was where he'd hidden everything. The torn-up cushions from our normal couch bounced down on top of everything else. I could feel blood rushing to my face. I didn't even want to *look* at Ms. Willard. We were so busted. We were *beyond* busted.

Without hesitating, Leaf rushed over and began furiously stuffing all the garbage back in the closet. Once I managed to get a grip on myself, I started helping too.

"We never have gotten around to cleaning out this closet," he said quickly. He grabbed the sailfish and threw it back inside.

"It's quite all right," Ms. Willard said.

Leaf and I exchanged a glance. Then I turned to her. She didn't look very happy—but she didn't look particularly angry either. She just looked a little tired, like she'd seen this kind of thing all the time.

"Have a seat, boys," she instructed.

We left the mess on the floor and returned to the easy chairs as fast as we could.

Ms. Willard sighed. "There's just one more thing I want to know," she said. "Leaf, tell me about how you think Blue managed to turn his schoolwork around."

"Well." Leaf took a long, slow breath. "Blue's a pretty smart guy, but he needs to work a little harder. He's, uh, spending more time doing his homework these days." He glanced at me. I nodded encouragingly—but just barely, so the social worker wouldn't see.

"Leaf checks my assignments," I added.

"Right," Leaf agreed.

Ms. Willard stood up and smoothed out the skirt of her suit, then she gave us a warm smile. "Fine, then. There are issues you two need to work on, but it's obvious how devoted you are to each other, and that's a bond I would never interfere with." She nodded toward the pile on the floor. "Anyone who would turn their house upside down just to impress me must really want to stay together. That's just the kind of environment I wish everyone had."

I just stared at her. That was it? After all the stress . . . and *everything*? It seemed so easy. On the other hand, though, I knew it wasn't. Convincing her that Leaf and I belonged together had taken a lot of hard work. On *both* of our parts.

Leaf stood and shook hands with Ms. Willard. "Thanks a lot."

"My pleasure." Ms. Willard headed for the front door. Leaf followed her. She opened the door and then stopped and turned toward me.

"I'm going to be keeping tabs on you for a while, Blue. I've talked with your teachers, and you've been doing much better this past week. But don't think you can let those grades slide again. I'll be checking back with your teachers."

"No, ma'am," I said.

"Good-bye, then." She smiled again and closed the door gently behind her.

Leaf and I just stared at each other while we listened to the sounds of her getting into her car and starting the engine. I literally felt like I was going to explode. But I also felt like all the tension of the past week had drained right out of me. It was a weird combination. As soon as the car pulled away from the house, we both ran to each other and threw up a high five.

"Awesome, bro!" I cried.

"We did it!" Leaf shouted.

I shook my head and let out a deep, shaky breath. "Thanks, man," I said.

He shrugged. "Not a problem."

"No, really. Thanks for doing all this."

Leaf put his hands on my shoulders and looked me in the eye. "I told you I'd do whatever it takes to keep you. I meant it." He cocked his head. "So we're cool now?"

I grinned. "We're cool. I just—" I broke off, catching a glimpse of the clock in the living room. "Oh no! I am way late for the carnival. Can you give me a ride to school?"

"Sure." Leaf snickered. He didn't move.

I shook my head. "No. Really."

"Blue—it's okay, bro." He jerked a thumb toward the front door. "She's gone."

"But I really *am* on this committee that's getting ready for the carnival," I insisted, stamping my feet. "I promised I'd help."

Leaf peered at me as if I were crazy. Then he started cracking up.

"What?" I asked, but I couldn't help laughing too.

"Nothing. You just never cease to amaze me." He reached into his pocket and jiggled the car keys. "Let's hit the road."

Elizabeth

"Liz, phone," my brother, Steven, called up the stairs. "It's the geek police. You're hogging all the geekiness in Sweet Valley."

I rolled my eyes and picked up the phone. How funny. My brother is such a comedian. *Not.*

"Hello?" I answered.

"Where *are* you?"

I winced. It was Jessica. And she didn't sound happy.

"What do you mean?" I asked.

"We need those peacock feathers," she stated.

My nose wrinkled. "Blue didn't give them to you?"

"Blue?" Jessica cried. "Why would *he* have them?"

"I ran into him at the mall," I explained. "He said he was on his way to the gym, and he'd bring them for me. . . ." My voice trailed off. Why was I even bothering to tell her this? Blue obviously wasn't there. *What a jerk.* How could he do this?

"Okay, look," I said. "I'll get some more feathers and come over. Steven can drive me."

"Okay. Hurry!" She hung up.

No time for a *Zone* meeting now, I realized. I dialed Anna's number. No one was home, so I left a message. "Hi, Anna. I can't make it to Vito's today. Blue promised he'd help me with something, but he flaked out on me, and now I have to deal with it. Sorry. Oh, and could you call Brian and Salvador and let them know? I'm in kind of a hurry. I'll see you at the gym. Bye."

I slammed down the phone. Now, thanks to Blue, Jessica was mad, and I'd had to change all my plans with my friends. My *real* friends. My reliable, responsible, dependable friends.

Well, I knew one thing. Whatever had been stressing Blue out clearly wasn't stressing him out anymore. Nope. He was back to blowing everything off again. How could I have ever felt sorry for him in the first place?

Brian

There was no way I could write this paper. I didn't even know how to *start*. I'd been staring at the blank page for almost twenty minutes now . . . but all I could think of was Kristin. All I could think of was how I should be with her. How I should be helping out with the carnival. Like I'd promised. It made me sick. Even worse, I'd agreed to go to a *Zone* meeting instead of going to the carnival preparations.

Kristin is always so ready to help everybody else all the time. And this carnival was practically the biggest thing in the world to her. And what did I do? I told her not to stress. Then I ignored her to hang out with my new friends.

The phone rang. My heart jumped. Maybe it was her. Maybe I could finally make up for being such a jerk. I snatched the receiver off the hook before the second ring.

"Hello?" I answered eagerly.

"Hey, it's Anna. Elizabeth left me a message.

She can't make our *Zone* meeting, so we're canceling."

I sighed, actually very relieved. "That's okay." I sat up straight. This could help me out, big time. "I was thinking about heading over to the gym to help set up for the carnival anyway."

"Me too. I think it would be fun," she said. "Salvador will probably come too. I'm going to ask my mom for a ride—do you need one?"

"No thanks," I answered. "My brother's going out anyway."

"Okay, see you there," she said. "Bye."

"Bye." I put down the phone. I was almost afraid to see Kristin. She'd be mad, for sure. But even if she yelled at me, I deserved it. I deserved whatever I had coming to me.

So. The question was: What could I do to patch things up? I'd been so caught up with three-headed reptiles and surfing and all the rest of it that I'd completely forgotten about my girl-friend. My amazing, special, wonderful, beautiful girlfriend. They didn't sell enough flowers at The Flower Bucket to make up for what I'd done.

No. I'd have to be creative. *Very* creative.

Kristin

"Hey, Kristin," Mark Elkins called to me from across the gym. "The ring-toss booth won't fit next to the fortune-teller's tent unless we squish it in."

I rolled my eyes. "So squish it," I yelled back. *Duh.* My patience was gone. Why had I ever *thought* that being in charge of the carnival would be fun?

People were going to start showing up at any minute. I doubted we'd be ready. Why *would* we be? Everybody was letting us down.

Like Brian Rainey, for instance.

Don't think about him, I told myself. If I thought about him, I'd start screaming or crying. No way. I had more important things to worry about.

A plain cardboard box sat next to a big roll of tickets for the raffle. I ripped it open to see what was inside and saw white paper tubes for the cotton-candy machine. If Brian were here, I could ask him to help me with this stuff. But he wasn't. I shoved the box of tubes next to an extra bag of plastic cups. Maybe I could find *somebody*. I glanced up toward the entrance of the gym.

My breath caught in my throat.

Brian.

At first I thought I was seeing things. But it was him, all right. He stood there in the doorway, with his hands in his pockets. He was looking out over the room, as if he wasn't quite sure what to do.

Then he smiled at me.

Part of me wanted to smile back. A very small part. A much bigger part wanted to punch him. And still another part was melting inside because he'd actually come. Why did he make my life so confusing?

I turned my attention back to the box, but I secretly watched him out of the corner of my eye as he walked up to me.

He cleared his throat.

"Yes?" I said, like I was really busy. Which I *was*.

"So, uh, what can I do to help?" he asked quietly.

Tell me how sorry you are and that you'll never blow me off for Blue Spiccoli again, I wanted to say. Which, of course, I didn't. I ran my finger down the list on my clipboard. "Bring this box of tubes to the cotton-candy machine," I said stiffly.

"Okay." He smiled at me one more time, then grabbed the box and headed for the far corner of the gym.

Now I couldn't concentrate. My brain was totally shot. The funny thing was, I was really relieved Brian had actually come, but he had me so confused right now that he probably would have helped me more if he'd stayed away. *Argh.* It wasn't fair!

Music suddenly filled the gym.

Good, I thought. Pete Coulter's brother had found a place to plug in his karaoke machine. That should help keep people energized. My eyes wandered up to the clock above the basketball hoop. Then I gasped. It was time! Time to open the carnival. My feet hurt already from standing up all day, but I didn't care. I glanced around. Amazingly, the game booths were all set up. Music was playing. The food smelled terrific. Almost everything was in place. Somehow we'd managed to get everything done.

Without Brian's help.

All of a sudden the music stopped.

I glanced over toward the karaoke machine. Pete Coulter was running up to me. "Kristin, could you come check out the video? There's something wrong with it."

I sighed. "Sure," I said, following him to the booth.

He fiddled with the buttons on the TV that played the lip-synch videos. For some reason, Brian appeared on the screen, holding a lop-sided paper heart over his chest and dancing. I frowned. He and Pete must have been testing the machine. Then Pete turned up the volume on the music.

My heart skipped a beat.

The song was "Say You Do," the first one Brian and I had ever slow danced to.

Brian waved at me from the TV. I waved back and laughed. He really had an awful voice. And he danced like a complete dork. But he sure was an adorable dork. It's hard to stay angry at somebody that cute. And that sweet.

As the last chorus played, Brian poked his head out between the curtains at the back of the booth. He grinned at me.

"I wouldn't send that tape to MTV just yet," I warned him, but I was smiling.

He pretended to be disappointed. "You don't think?"

"Um, no."

He held out his hand to me. I took it in mine. It was warm and comforting. Like always.

Our eyes locked together.

"I'm sorry—," we both started at the same time.

141

I giggled and squeezed his hand. "It's okay," I said.

"You sure? I've been totally . . ."

I shook my head. "Positive."

He started tugging me away from the karaoke booth. "I'm starving. Can I buy you some nachos, you know, to make up for everything?"

You already did make up for everything, I thought. But of course, I didn't say that. I was starving. I nodded. "Yes, you can."

Bethel

"This is going to be ugly," I said to my boyfriend, Jameel. We were watching a group of eighth-grade boys lining up to try and knock our principal, Mr. Todd, into the dunk tank.

Jameel smirked. "At least he should float okay."

"Definitely," I agreed. Mr. Todd isn't the skinniest guy around.

The first two guys struck out. Jameel yawned. "Let's play something," he suggested.

"Sure." I glanced around the crowded gym. It seemed like everybody in the school was there. I pointed over to where a football player was being helped into a suit made out of Velcro, getting ready to trampoline up onto the big Velcro wall. "Let's try that."

"Nah . . . let's win something first. Hey, that looks good." He pointed at the shoot-a-bug game. "I want to win you one of those blue bears."

Great. Just what I needed. A four-foot-tall blue teddy bear. Must be a guy thing, I decided. Every guy thinks he has to win his girlfriend a stuffed animal.

We headed past the fortune-teller's tent and a soda-can car-racing booth. Jameel checked out the little race cars but shook his head.

He dragged me over to the shooting booth.

I groaned to myself when I saw who was there.

It was Lacey and that ridiculous boyfriend of hers, Gel. *Uh-oh,* I thought. Gel was getting ready to shoot, and Lacey was standing back a few feet, watching him. She looked over her shoulder when she heard us walk up.

I kept my expression blank. Would she ignore me? Glare at me? Put me down? Now that her crisis had passed, she probably had forgotten all about the help I gave her.

"Hey," she said.

I nodded back. "Hey."

She pointed at my bell-bottom jeans. "Nice pants," she remarked.

For a moment I analyzed what she'd said. She didn't sound sarcastic. Or mean. Or like she had a hidden agenda. In fact, she just sounded like she liked my jeans. Which would be a first.

She must have caught the expression on my

face because she smiled. "No, really. They're cool."

I shrugged. "Thanks." My jeans might be cool—but not as cool as her outfit. Baggy black pants pulled in at the waist with a black belt and a tight, neon green top that stopped just above her belly button, and about ten black rubber bracelets on her wrist. Even her eyes were ringed in black eyeliner. But that was Lacey Frells. Nobody dressed as hip.

"Check this out," Gel said to Jameel, and squeezed off a shot.

None of the bug targets fell down.

Jameel smiled. "Watch this, hotshot." He raised his gun, spread his legs wide, and fired. With a *plink* the caterpillar figure fell backward. "You gotta lock your elbows," he told Gel.

Gel hefted his pistol. "Really?" He sighted down the barrel, copying Jameel's stance.

Lacey snorted. "Are those two lame or what?"

I watched Gel line up a shot. His tongue was sticking out of his mouth. And it was wiggling.

"Beyond lame," I agreed.

"Totally." She rolled her eyes. Then she gave me a smile. A genuine smile. "Good thing we're not guys, huh?"

I smiled back. "Good thing."

It was a good thing we weren't total enemies anymore either.

Elizabeth

How could it be that of all the booths at the carnival, Blue got assigned to run the tip-a-troll game with me? I didn't even want to *look* at him, let alone talk to him. He'd blown Jessica off, and now he was acting like nothing was wrong. Then he came late with his *own* bag of feathers. As if it even mattered. And now I was stuck in this teeny little booth with him for a whole hour, taking tickets and watching people trying to knock these little creatures over with beanbags. What fun.

"They get three beanbags for one ticket, right?" he asked me.

"That's what Kristin told us," I muttered.

Ronald Rheece walked up to the booth, carrying a candy apple.

Blue grinned at him. "Hey, dude. You ready for this?"

Ronald nodded seriously. "Yes."

I leaned forward to take his ticket, and my hair fell forward, covering my face. When I went to straighten up, it was stuck on his candy apple. "Oh no," I cried.

I fumbled with my fingers to try and untangle myself but couldn't see what I was doing, and I was just making it worse. Why did disaster always seem to strike whenever Ronald was near?

Ronald tried to pull the apple away, but my hair came with it.

"Ouch!" I yelled.

"Whoa, Ronald!" Blue cried. "Hang on there."

"I'm sorry, Elizabeth," Ronald apologized. "It seems that we've created quite a strong chemical bond."

"Right," I snapped from behind my candied hair. I wasn't exactly in the mood to talk about the scientific elements of our problem.

I could hear Blue chuckling.

"Hold still," he commanded. "I'll fix this."

He had to stand so close that I could feel his breath on the back of my neck. Very quickly he separated my hair from the apple. I *was* mad at him, but still . . . I kind of liked him there, right next to me. Did that make any sense? I sighed. Of course not. *Nothing* made sense when it came to Blue Spiccoli and me.

"Okay," he said finally. "All done."

"Thanks," I told Blue.

"I'll go get some soap," Ronald mumbled, and scurried away.

Elizabeth

I straightened, feeling the sticky goo glopped in my hair. "Ick. I should go clean up."

Blue grinned. "No, don't. I love the smell of candy apples."

I wrinkled my nose. "Really?"

"I'm serious. Totally. It reminds me of my mom and dad. They used to take Leaf and me to this amusement park all the time. . . ." His voice trailed off. He had a distant look in his eyes. Then he sighed and shook his head.

I bit my lip. I'd never heard him talk about his parents before. My throat tightened. It was so easy to forget that Blue had lost his mom and dad. He always acted so positive. He never wanted anyone to feel sorry for him. I couldn't even *imagine* what it would be like to experience the loss of even *one* parent.

Blue gave me a little grin. "Hey, I didn't mean to bum you out."

I tried to smile. "You didn't. It's just . . ." I had no idea what I wanted to say.

"Elizabeth?" he asked quietly.

I nodded.

"I'm sorry I freaked out on you last night," he murmured. "I've kind of got a lot of stuff on my mind, but I shouldn't have yelled at you. That was completely uncool."

I shook my head. I felt like a weight had been

lifted off my chest. Blue's life couldn't be more different than mine. And maybe I shouldn't expect the same things of him that I did of other people. "No, that's okay. I shouldn't have yelled at you either. Anyway, you brought the feathers. That's what counts."

Blue heaved a big sigh. He ran his hand over his short hair. "You know Leaf is my legal guardian, right?"

I nodded tentatively. "Uh-huh."

"Well, the reason I was acting so weird is because, see, social services checks up on us sometimes to make sure Leaf's being a good parent and stuff. And I've been blowing off school this whole semester. I mean, my best grade was a C. My new social worker found out, and I guess she got all concerned, so she decided to do a visit and see what was going on with me." He cleared his throat. "She came over today, as a matter of fact."

Wow. My heart was pounding. Everything suddenly fell into place. No wonder he'd been freaking out about keeping his house clean. No wonder he'd been acting so stressed. And joining every club under the sun. And worrying about his homework on a Friday night.

"I've been such a jerk," I found myself saying. Blue had all these problems—and all I could think about was how his behavior affected *me*. And my good time.

"No, you weren't," Blue replied softly. "*I* was the one who was being weird. I was just totally sure the social worker would take me away from Leaf and make me live in a foster home unless I could prove I was like this incredibly amazing student."

I nodded. "So you ran around like crazy, trying to make everything right. And we never even noticed." I hung my head. "I'm really sorry."

Blue smiled. "Don't be. I'm the one who should be sorry."

"But—"

"No, really," he interrupted. His blue eyes twinkled. "If I hadn't been so uptight, you might have ended up becoming a totally mellow surf chick."

I laughed. "Uh-oh. I don't know if I could have handled that."

His expression turned serious. He stepped closer to me. "So, are we friends?" he asked.

"Of course," I whispered. I didn't say anything else. I just stared into those amazing blue eyes of his. It wasn't hard to do.

Blue

Hardly anybody came to play tip-a-troll. But I didn't care. Hanging out with Elizabeth was good enough for me. It was almost time to go when this guy with dark, curly hair came up to us. I'd seen him around school before. He held out one of those white-and-red paper dishes. It was empty except for a slice of jalapeño pepper sitting in a little puddle of cheese at the bottom.

"Hey, Elizabeth," he said, looking a little embarrassed. "Anna told me to give you these nachos, but it took so long to find you, I already ate them."

Elizabeth rolled her eyes. "Thanks a lot, Salvador." She turned to me. "Salvador works on *Zone* with me," she explained.

I smiled at him. "That's cool."

"This is my good friend Blue," she said to him. "The difference between him and you is that *he* would have actually bought his own nachos instead of eating mine."

I didn't hear the rest of it. I couldn't listen. Because at that moment I felt like I was surfing a perfect, ten-foot wave. Elizabeth had called me her *good friend*. In that supercasual way . . . like it's just the way it is, like it's something you take for granted.

I'm her good friend.

Radical.

Completely, totally radical.

I watched her leaning over the counter, laughing at something Salvador said. Elizabeth Wakefield thought I was her good friend.

Sweet.

But not as sweet as it would be to be more than her good friend. I watched her eyes twinkle under the gym lights. She shook back her hair, completely forgetting about the big hunk of pink sugar stuck to the side.

Someday, I told myself. *Someday I'll be something more. . . .*

Check out the **all-new** ....

(**Sweet Valley Web site—**)

www.sweetvalley.com

New Features

Cool Prizes

The ONLY official Web site!

Hot Links

(And much more!)